Winter Lights

DEBORAH JENKINS

Fairlight Books

First published by Fairlight Books 2023

Fairlight Books
Summertown Pavilion, 18–24 Middle Way, Oxford,
OX2 7LG

A CIP catalogue record for this book is available from the
British Library.

1 2 3 4 5 6 7 8 9 10

ISBN 978-1-914148-57-6

www.fairlightbooks.com

Printed and bound in Great Britain

Designed by Rebecca Fish

To Mum, who always finds light in dark places.

The light shines in the darkness, and the darkness has not overcome it

— John 1:5 (The Bible, New International Version)

Spotify Playlist

Author's Note

While I was writing these stories, there was music in my head. This was a good thing as I wrote them during the summer when Christmas and New Year seemed as remote as a pair of colourful aunts you don't see that often. Listening to music helped me to get 'in the zone' when trying to paint word pictures for the season. Then it occurred to me that readers might enjoy the pieces I was listening to, so I offer them to you, one for each story. Think of it as a small gift for the time of year. And I hope you enjoy *Winter Lights*.

'The Key' – *Christmas Lights* (Coldplay)

'The End of the Line' – *All I Want for Christmas Is You* (Mariah Carey)

'Christmas at the Masala Ram' – *Tubular Bells* (Mike Oldfield)

'The Photo' – *Stand by Me* (Ben E. King)

'Once Did Orla Davis...' – *Once in Royal David's City* (Choir of King's College, Cambridge)

'The Chain' – *Driving Home for Christmas* (Chris Rea)

'The Gift' – *Carol of the Bells* (version by John Williams)

'Something for Yourself' – *Happy New Year* (Abba)

'Slowly Then All at Once' – *Cello Suite No. 1 in G Major* (J. S. Bach)

'Winter Lights' – *Auld Lang Syne* (Dougie MacLean)

The Key

As she turns the key in the ignition, Radio 2 blasts a morning welcome. Amy puts on her seatbelt and reverses down the drive. It's not yet seven, it's pitch black, and her brain is as fogged as the windscreen. Pulling a tissue from her pocket, she rubs at the glass weakly. She must get one of those shammy leathers that people keep in glove compartments, where they lead quiet lives when not in use.

I wish I was a shammy leather, she thinks.

Band Aid croons from the radio. She turns them off.

She backs into the road and the bumper nudges Rod-next-door's dustbin. *More haste, less speed.* Dad's favourite proverb. She watches in the glare of the headlights as the bin slow-motion-slides down the steep pavement, rocking with glee, as if this is its one chance of escape.

Amy swears, then winces. She is appalled at her language these days. But it's as if all the stress in her life – Mia, school, the sheer daily grind of Keeping Things Going – has stolen her good words and left the bad ones in charge.

The dustbin reaches the edge of the pavement, clips a lamppost and pirouettes onto the tarmac. The lid jerks open, and three badly secured bags of rubbish share their contents with the road. In the wing mirror, Amy glimpses unwashed cans and a Tena pad.

She wrenches the gearstick into neutral, kills the engine, leaps out, forgetting the belt. It's slack beneath her fingers.

Great. Something else to fix.

Curtains twitch along the length of the terrace. A bin lorry reverses around the corner, beeping. Amy strides towards the mess. She bends down and starts to rake the rubbish into the split bags with her fingers. It's a messy business – other people's waste is even worse than your own. By the time she's finished, her hands are covered in slime and on her jacket there's a drop of baked-bean juice. It's right next to the coffee stain from yesterday. She heaves the last sack into the bin and pushes it towards the pavement. She needs to jam her high-heeled shoe against the bottom to lever it into place. This is strangely satisfying.

At this point, she's panting. She pulls her sleeve back, lifting her arm to read the time in a circle of light. Her life, she decides, lurches from crisis to crisis – caring for Dad; Ofsted; Mia becoming a monster. And to top it off nicely, there's Christmas…

Mia! There's no sign of life from her room, her window a closed eye. She taps up the drive and jams her key in the lock.

Wrenching the door open, she leans in and shouts, 'Mia! It's twenty past! Are you up yet?'

There's a scuffle along the hall. Her daughter appears in her ratty dressing gown with a bowl of cereal. Her hair, in yesterday's plait, is matted. Her face is covered in kohl. She rolls her eyes.

'Course I'm up!' she says levelly. 'After your fight with a dustbin, the whole road is.'

Amy glares. She doesn't have time for this.

'You can get the back-door key from Rod,' she says shortly. 'I can't trust you with your own.' Her gloves are still on the hall table. She picks them up. Memories are everywhere in this house; even this table. The way Mum put candles here at Christmas. A candle carousel. As a child, she was allowed to light them. It was magical watching each tiny flame leap to life, fragile, flickering.

But together, as the hot air rose, the flames made the fan spin. She loved it, Mia loved it, but when Mum and Dad moved to the flat, it had gone astray.

Mia is watching her. Amy swallows.

As she closes the door she glimpses her daughter's face, and it catches her off guard. Tucked beneath the mutinous expression, there is the tiniest burst of sympathy.

The drive to school, between quiet fields, soothes her. Dawn hems the darkness; fog skims the trees. Every so often, light spills from a cottage window. From wrinkled ground beyond a hedge, there's a rise of birds, wings gilded by a fingertip of sun. And her heart cannot help but lift too. Above the fog, the sky is clear, a lovely day.

The car drives itself along the lanes which criss-cross this part of Sussex. What's she going to do about Mia? They've always done life together. Fleeting images kaleidoscope through her head: at four, Mia dancing in the sea; at ten, hiding in the library; and having their make-up done for her fifteenth birthday.

Then, at sixteen, overnight, wanting nothing to do with her. Just as Jack appears in her life. Jack, with his easy smile and too-blue eyes, good looking, self-assured. To say nothing of the fact that he reminds Amy of someone she was smitten with at that age...

She takes a long breath and tries to focus on what's ahead: the interviews, the data, the staff meeting. She had never wanted to be a deputy head, preferring the children, the thrill of 'Oh-I-get-it-now!' But when the old deputy retired and she was offered a promotion, she'd had to accept. Because that's what you do when worrying about money is as natural for you as breathing.

Of course, it's only temporary and she's not sure whether to apply for it long-term, but the job is in some way her salvation.

A place where she has no choice but to be focused on the here and now. At work, there's no time to think about home life, where she's constantly failing. School is something she's good at. And the distance from home allows her to put on another persona: calm, controlled, capable. The car gobbles the road, each mile a step closer in that effortless slide into an efficient version of herself, complete by the time she turns into the school car park.

The stress of it is not good, though – she knows this. An endless parade of complaints; a bottomless inbox; policies, planning, data. And that's without Ofsted hovering, determined to bring them down. She deals with problems non-stop for twelve hours. She eats her lunch to the click of emails, interruptions. It's rare to get fifteen minutes to herself each day. And wakeful nights do nothing to energise her for the next one.

But there are only three sleeps until the end of term. Then three more to do something about Christmas.

She is a survivor, she knows this. *You can do this, Amy!* echoes in her head. She has heard it often enough from friends and family that she almost believes it herself. Miss Amy Lane is a coper. But coping is not living. Coping is lurching from one crisis to the next, shutting off your feelings and distancing yourself from your life as much as you can. Then you can use logic to solve its problems. Sorry, *challenges*. You're not allowed to call them problems any more.

She thinks briefly of yesterday's: Mia losing the key. Their new front door was a luxury, but when the old one finally splintered, slammed after a row, Amy had had no choice. She can't even remember what the row was about; the door-splitting erased it completely.

'Are you sure?' the salesman had asked her. 'It's good quality for a good price, but they make their money in other ways.

Like replacement keys – they cost a fortune.' The bloke had a kind face and honest eyes. She remembers this. She also remembers that, as ever, she was in a hurry, to get away, to get on. But if she'd thought about it for one moment, she would have demurred; she would have known. Mia is always losing things. Last night's angry protestations echo in her head ('You never *gave* me the key, Mum. So how could I lose it?') but Amy doesn't believe her. She remembers showing it to her, explaining how valuable it was, how Mia must absolutely never lose it. She once trusted her daughter with everything. But since Jack, she has no faith in anything.

The lane zigzags through trees towards the sun. She lifts her face, greedy for its warmth. *Close your eyes to your problems, but they'll be there when you open them.* She blinks at the memory. *Go away, Dad!* It occurs to her that he is one of her problems now. But she loves him; of course she does. She'd do anything for him, however bad the motor neurone disease gets – make meals, get him dressed, help him in the bathroom. She will try to pop in on him on the way home.

She thanks God for her brother, who does so much for Dad – but after all, Aidan's a vicar. That's the job, isn't it? Strange – she always thought she was the strong one. Now she's not so sure. Her twin, for all his timid ways, has found a contentment she can only dream of. Perhaps she's been wrong all these years, to associate lack of ambition with cowardice. Faith, after all, demands a particular kind of courage.

Then there's their little sister Anna's baby. God knows when she'll have time to visit the new arrival, or her friend, Jan, whose husband is ill. She feels such a bad person not having time for them.

When the tractor hits, she's thinking about Mum: how Mum would have told her not to take the deputy job. *There are always*

ways to make money, but you can never get the time back. Mum liked soundbites, too, but hers were wiser, inviting themselves in before you could shut the door. If only she were here now. The road stretches ahead emptily. Amy closes her eyes for a second, sun on skin.

The first thing she notices is the noise. That sound of folding metal, scream upon scream of it, scraping itself against and around her like a tortured animal. Then, movement, as she's hurled through the air, an arm twisted painfully behind her. After that, silence.

Lying on the cold earth, her eyes to the sky, she sees birds circling. Perhaps they think she's dead. Perhaps she is dead. *Oh God, don't let me be dead... And sorry for the swears*, she adds, in case it counts.

A pungent smell of manure invades her throat. *Not dead, then.* In the distance, there's the hum of a plane. She turns her head to one side and sees it climb, steep and slow, above apricot-coloured clouds. How strange, thinks her shell-shocked brain, that people are up there, safe inside a metal can with nothing beneath them but sky. But here the sky is above her, yawning, endless, a perfect dome of yearning blue, and she, on solid ground, is not safe at all.

It strikes her, as it did after Mum's death, how short life is, how fragile. A brief dance with pain and passion, then a lying down, a rejoining, sewn back into the earth from which we came. She begins to shake.

Now, Amy, get a grip! She moves her arms and legs experimentally, tries to steady herself. Her right arm aches from being pinned behind her on impact. Apart from this, she feels OK. She tries to sit up. Her side throbs and there's a dull ache in her leg. She leans on the other arm to lever herself up. She can hear her breath loud and fast. The supporting arm begins to shake uncontrollably. She supposes it's the shock. She rolls one leg under her, tries to stand, but a squelching noise distracts her. She looks up.

A woman is marching across the field towards her. She's wearing dungarees, a jacket, wellies. The wet soil submits to her ample stride, sliding away either side of her like parting waves. When she gets to Amy, she bends down.

'Are you alright? I thought you were a goner there.' A ponytail swings over her shoulder as she examines Amy's face.

'You've cut yourself,' she says. 'Does it hurt?'

Amy frowns and reaches up to touch her face. Her hand comes away bright and livid, a scream of red between the pastels of earth and sky.

'What's your name? How do you feel? Do you want to try and get up?' asks the woman. She is not young, but her eyes dance with concern.

'I'm Amy.' She cannot stop shaking. Her voice sounds croaky in the cool air.

The woman takes off her jacket and wraps it around Amy's shoulders.

'I'm Steph. You just hit my tractor, and you're shaking,' she says. 'It's the shock and the cold. I need to get you to the house. Can you stand up?'

Amy tries to stand but her legs feel wobbly and strange. The woman is tall and strong. She helps lift Amy to her feet to rehearse a few cautious steps. Her heels sink into the soil.

'Take them off?' says Steph. She leans down and eases each leg out of its shoe. The wet earth slides up Amy's stockinged feet. It is very cold. With some part of her brain, she is thinking about the expression 'teeth chattering with cold'. She can understand it now.

Step by step, they inch their way across the field towards the gate. Steph is slow, patient. As they get closer, they can walk in the deep ruts made by tractor wheels. Amy glances back at her shoes. The red heels sit wonkily in mud, out of place in their new surroundings.

'You were incredibly lucky,' says Steph, shifting her weight so she can take more of Amy's. 'You're in shock but don't seem badly hurt. I forgot my mobile – dammit – but once we get to the farmhouse, I'll ring for an ambulance so they can check you over.'

Amy stops walking. 'Oh no,' she says. 'I'm sure I'll be fine. I must get to school. I have a busy day.'

Later, she can't believe she thought this a serious option. She was clearly not quite with it. How could she have imagined after such a serious accident that her day would carry on as normal? But shock numbs us. It takes away our ability to reason, to see the obvious. She will never forget Steph's words, her kindness, her generous way of bringing her down to earth.

'You've had an accident, Amy,' she says. 'It's hard to think straight when things like this happen. But you're probably not going to work today. You need to be checked over and rest until you're better. When we get home, let me know who I can ring.'

Amy stares through the gate towards the lane. She can see the corner of her car. Its bumper is ripped off. The windscreen has smashed, and the roof has buckled, with a large hole on the driver's side. She must have been catapulted through it by the force of the impact.

She gives a small sob. Steph tightens her grip and pulls a tissue from her pocket. Her voice is reassuring.

'Amy, we need to get you to the house,' she says. 'Don't look at the car. It's in a bad way but you're going to be fine, and that's the main thing.'

Amy nods, tears sliding down her face. Why does everything she touch turn bad? She can't even drive to school safely. Miss Lane – efficient, controlled – is not here today. As they shuffle through the gate, she turns her head so she can see Steph's face. Her rescuer has sturdy features. It's the face of a person who knows who she is, where she's going.

'Why aren't you angry with me?' Amy asks her between sniffs. 'I just collided head-on with your tractor.'

They limp through the last set of ruts. The open gate is tied to a post with blue string. They turn into the lane and Amy sees the extent of the devastation which used to be her car. She cannot believe that minutes ago it was a moving object. It's hard to imagine anyone sitting in it, let alone driving it. There is nothing left of its original shape and if she hadn't been thrown out on impact, she'd be dead.

'That's why,' says Steph softly, nodding towards the tractor. She sounds apologetic.

The tractor sits, ponderous, beneath a tree whose bare arms droop from sleeves of mistletoe.

There's not a scratch on it.

They arrive at the farmhouse, a shuffle past the tractor and along the lane. Steph sits her in front of the wood burner with a blanket. She makes them both coffee laced with whisky and a bowl of porridge. To Amy's surprise, she devours it. After the row about the key last night, she had slept badly and woken late. She nags Mia about breakfast but it's a luxury she herself can rarely afford.

Steph takes the phone into the other room to ring the paramedics, the police, the school. Amy leans back on the sofa and remembers how to breathe. The room is a kind of all-purpose space with a kitchen at one end – a range and wooden counters with cast-iron handles – and a sitting room at the other. This contains aged sofas, their innards spilling out, a Turkish rug and a wood burner. At the centre of the room is a huge slab of wood surrounded by mismatched chairs at various angles. In the middle of this table is a bowl of holly. Apart from this, there's no evidence of Christmas. *Glad I'm not the only one*, she thinks. She is increasingly unable to ignore her neighbour's sparkles, Rod's vibrating Santa.

An aged dog lies in a basket by the fire. Having lifted its head dozily as they entered, it takes no notice of her.

It is very quiet. Just the hiss of scorched wood, distant birds, Steph's voice from the other room. Amy slows her breathing, the way she's learned to – slow in-breath, slower out-breath. Suddenly she feels very tired. She closes her eyes, tries to process the last twenty-four hours: a difficult day at school, a quick visit with Dad. Then, Mia and Jack wrapped around each other on the sofa. Followed by the key.

I gave it to you!

You didn't! You showed it to me. You talked about giving it to me but that's all!

Well, where is it, then?

I don't know, Mum! I'm not a mind reader!

Then this morning, oversleeping, the dustbin, the crash...

Her eyes snap open as Steph comes in. She is still on the phone. 'Can you answer a few questions?'

Amy nods.

'Are you breathing easily?'

'Yes.'

'Do you feel dizzy?'

'No.'

'Where's the pain?'

'Erm.' Amy traces the lines of her body like a map. 'Aching arm, aching leg, feel a bit weak.'

Steph repeats each answer into the phone, speaks with the operator, finishes the call.

'Right!' she says. 'A first responder is on the way, as are the police. But that could take a while. I've rung the school. I need to move the tractor now. It's blocking the lane. Your car, thank God, is near enough to the hedge for people to pass. You're not the only one who uses the lane as a rat run!'

With two brisk movements, she grabs her keys and pulls on her wellies.

'I won't be long,' she says over her shoulder. She slams the door behind her.

Amy leans back and lets the silence fill her, takes slow breaths. She has no choice but to accept things as they are: her car is a write-off, she can't go to school, she must wait for the responder. Mia doesn't know so she needn't worry about her yet. The carers will be in for Dad so there's no rush there. She wonders if her phone will be recovered from the car. It's strange to have any length of time without it.

She looks out of the window across fields. There's a barn in the distance, a clutch of trees. The sky is indigo blue, the sun winter-pale. A blackbird lands on the windowsill. It observes her, jerking its head from side to side, its eyes rimmed with circles of topaz. She has never noticed this before. But then she can't remember when she last sat this still, and looked. She reaches into her pocket for a tissue and her fingers close around something. She pulls out the key.

When Steph gets back, stamping her boots on the copious doormat which fills a good part of the room, Amy is sobbing.

'Hey!' she cries. 'What happened?' She grabs a box from the kitchen and lurches across the rug, pulling out too many tissues. She sinks into the chair opposite and puts them in Amy's lap.

'I'm a terrible mother,' Amy gulps. There is a beat.

'Aren't we all?' says Steph, but it's not a question. Amy looks at her over the tissue covering her face. Steph is leaning back in the chair, watching her. 'How many do you have?'

'Children?' Amy blows her nose and is concerned to see blood.

'Daughters,' says Steph. 'I assume that's what you're talking about?'

Amy gapes, which is hard when you're squeezing the bridge of your nose. 'How did you know?'

Steph gives a barking laugh. 'Children are carved from our very souls, but they grow up and want to find their own way. Sons make us let them go but daughters can't.'

Amy puts the tissue down. 'Mia is my only child,' she says. 'My mother was older when she had me, so we weren't close when I was little. But Mia and I, we've been everything to each other. She's sixteen now and pulling away. I... I hate it! Added to which, I accused her of losing this key. I was horrible to her.'

She holds it up. It really is the most ridiculous thing she has ever seen – wide and shiny and long. How could she not have felt it in her pocket?

'We often run from those we need the most.' Steph is looking into the fire.

'Sorry?'

'Something my mother used to say...' Steph gives herself a shake. 'I have three daughters and a son,' she says, 'and they're everything to me, too. But they have their own lives and I have mine. Their father left me, so I manage the farm now. It keeps me busy and, in the main, happy.'

Amy's mouth falls open. 'You run this farm? On your own?'

Steph shrugs. 'It was my parents' farm; I grew up here. It's part of who I am. I wasn't going to give it up for a divorce!'

A silence as Amy digests these words. At least it's taking her mind off the accident. But how could this woman run a farm on her own? She pulls the blanket around her and studies Steph's face. She is watching the fire, averting her gaze, but Amy sees it, the sadness belying her words. She looks down at the key, twisting beneath her fingers. Life, she thinks, has a way of humbling us all.

Outside there is the sound of an engine, the slam of a door. In the corner of the window, she can see a man in a fluorescent jacket.

'They're here,' says Steph. She gets up, pulls dog hair from her sleeve, smiles. She looks down at Amy. 'Your Mia is sixteen. She wants to be an adult. Let her! In many cultures, adulthood is acknowledged at puberty.'

Amy thinks of all the things she can't trust her daughter with. She opens her mouth. 'But...'

Outside, there's the sound of footsteps, a cough. Steph pushes her hair over her shoulder.

'The key is to believe in them. They need that. When they're small, they trust you to look after them, to be in charge, and somehow, you manage it. When they're older, you return the favour.'

A knock on the door. 'And if you don't let them make mistakes,' she adds, as she picks up the tissue box, 'they'll count yours, forever...'

It is a long day and by the time everything's done, it's the afternoon. Amy has been checked over and given a list of symptoms to look for. The police have come and asked questions and filled out reports; arrangements have been made to move her wreck of a car. Steph has made more coffee and then sandwiches, stacked up the fire, come and gone.

Eventually, the light begins to fade, and a cold moon hangs across the fields, slung low like a dropped coin. The police take her home.

'I have no words,' Amy tells Steph as they hug.

'You would have done the same,' she says. 'Go lightly, remember?'

Mia cries and hugs her and says she could have lost her. She makes them a pasta supper. Then they curl up on the sofa like they used to. She tells Amy she knows she's been a cow lately and she's sorry, but she might be again. Amy says she's the one who should be sorry and tells her about the key (she might do this again too). They laugh.

Then Mia says she has something to show her. 'It's for Christmas,' she says.

Amy raises her eyebrows and listens to prolonged scuffling in the other room. When she is finally summoned, the hall is dark but in the light from the kitchen, it sits where it always sat.

'Oh, my goodness, where...?'

'I made it, in D and T. I copied it from a photo of Grandad's.'

Amy admires the candle carousel in the half darkness. 'How on earth did you do it? It's so intricate, so clever!'

'Jack helped me.' Mia's eyes are bright, hopeful. 'He's a good guy, Mum. You should give him a chance!'

Amy takes a breath. 'I don't trust him. And I don't trust you when you're with him.'

(This is what she wants to say.)

But instead, she reaches for the small box. She takes a match and strikes it, touches the first candle. A tiny burst, a tremble of light, and then the flame, sharp and strong. One by one, she lights them all.

And as the wooden blades begin to spin, her eyes meet Mia's, and she knows they're both remembering what Gran used to say.

May there be light for you in dark places when all other lights go out.

Amy takes the key from her pocket and puts it on the table.

'This is for you,' she says.

The End of the Line

The moment she steps from the train station into rain, she remembers. You know that thing? You think you've forgotten something because, when you left home, you were carrying a parcel/library book/gift. But you've delivered it now. With a rush of relief, you relax.

Well, this isn't that thing. This is another thing, where a lingering sense of unease – you should be holding something, apart from your umbrella and copy of the London *Metro* – turns out to be true.

It hits Kate as she hovers at the edge of the road outside the station. Christmas lights spill across puddles. Rain treads lightly on silver. Nearby, someone is selling chestnuts. A man pushes past shouting 'Got some!' into his phone. A pack of wrapping paper is sticking out from under his arm, catching her on the cheek. She winces. Then, tossing the *Metro* onto a bench, she races back to the train. This takes her less time than you'd think as there is only one platform. It's a country station, the end of the line, and in about ten minutes the train will amble back between quiet fields towards London.

She is out of breath by the time she gets there. Most of the arrivals have dispersed, swallowed by cars or taxis or a parking space the other side of the road. At the other end of the platform, a man is levering a suitcase onto the train. He's wearing a mask with a Santa beard. Nearby, a youth, in an overfull rucksack, is unlocking his bike. He bends to put on bicycle clips and the bag bulges ahead of her. She swerves and glares, but he's oblivious, earphones in, his back to her.

Kate takes all this in with one half of her brain as she runs through puddles, wetting her leggings and too-short boots. Why hadn't she worn her mac, for pity's sake? She lopes, panting, along the platform, trying to remember which carriage she was in. The one near the bench, wasn't it? Or was it by the ticket-office? *Aaargh!* She runs back, presses the button, enters further up the train. She barrels through carriages, rucksack bouncing, hair flying, eyes running across the left-hand seats. People look up from their phones, stare. She doesn't care. There aren't many of them anyway. It's the end of the line.

She pauses, gasping, next to two women sitting where she thinks she was seated.

'Did you... Was there... I left a parcel here. Did you see it?'

They gawp at her, shaking heads. One of them is wearing head-phones. She starts to say it again.

'No, love, sorry,' the other one replies, 'there was nothing here.' She has heavily made-up eyes and there's lipstick on her teeth.

Kate nods and keeps going. She passes only a handful of people from then on and, to her relief, doesn't know any of them. It is a small town; everyone knows everyone. It's when she's halfway through the last carriage that the train starts moving. *Oh no! No-no-no-no!* Then she remembers. They were late out of London Bridge (leaves on the line) so they had arrived later than usual. The train would not have its usual ten-minute rest before trundling back. She had rung to let Pat know but no one had picked up, so she'd left a message.

'Hi Pat, the train is late. I hope Meg doesn't have a wobbly. I've got the present, wrapped in her favourite shiny paper too. But don't tell her, obviously. I'm just so relieved it's arrived in time. I'll get to The Heights as soon as I can.'

An image of Megan rears up before her, in her chair by the window, watching the drive, the clock. Waiting. The train gathers speed. She reaches the guard's van, which is empty. There are no guards on the late trains. The present has been stolen and she has nothing for Megan at Christmas.

Come to think of it, she remembers someone in the seat behind, leaning and staring while she was on the phone. She had not looked round but sensed curious eyes. Perhaps that person took it.

Anyway, there it is. The gift has gone, and she will have to get off at Eastleigh and get a taxi back to Henford, as the next train will be in an hour. Kate throws herself into a seat, wetly. She hadn't even had time to put up her umbrella. Despair slinks into the seat beside her.

'You're so useless!' it says. 'You can't even remember to take all your stuff with you!'

What can she say? It's true.

'You were a bad daughter and you're a bad sister...' Kate gives a small sob to acknowledge this.

'It was stupid enough to have such an expensive gift made, on a whim. But then to lose it...'

Her grip tightens around the rucksack on her knee. Tears somersault down, softening the black fabric.

'It's just been the most awful year,' she reminds Despair. 'Mum dying; Megan going into care; stress at work...'

She tails off. Despair watches, with raised eyebrows. 'So? Other people have stuff too. And they cope. They get tough, they get through.'

She considers this. The rhythm of the train is strangely calming as it rocks from side to side in the darkness. Through the window, she can see houses lit up for Christmas: windows picked out in lights, open curtains. She cranes her head to catch a glimpse of lamplight, a glistening tree. She sighs.

'It's Christmas in two days and you haven't even got a tree or gone shopping!'

This is true, but there hadn't seemed much point. She is planning to buy flowers for the day itself and the only person she needs a present for is Megan.

She sighs and takes out her phone, clicks on the camera icon, reverses it. Her face, pale and blotchy, stares back tiredly. She hadn't had time to wash her hair before work, pulling it back with a clip so you could clearly see, in the hollows and lines of her face, the sadness gathered. She should have put on make-up.

'You look like a child,' scoffs Despair. 'An elderly child!' It stretches and settles, watching her with hungry eyes.

'*This train,*' says the announcement, '*is the Southern service to London Bridge, calling at Eastleigh, Monksted, Hillborough, Faridge, Cleaver...*' Kate closes her eyes and lets the familiar list roll over her. Its musicality is soothing and takes her mind off Despair and its killer observations.

The train lumbers on. Rain slaps on windows. Night settles in. She stares out at the darkness, straining her eyes for pinpricks of light. She likes to think of people getting ready for Christmas, wrapping gifts, decorating the tree. Like she used to.

'*...and London Bridge,*' concludes the announcer with a lip-smack.

'And then back,' adds Kate, 'to us, at the end of the line.' She glances at Despair, who gives a satisfied nod.

The train begins to slow as they approach Eastleigh. Kate looks up, looks round. There is no one else at her end of the carriage. She sighs, takes a breath, wipes her eyes with her sleeve. The train brakes. Nudging Despair aside, she stands up and with bent-kneed gracelessness, eases her way into the aisle.

She stares at the floor as she lurches towards the doors. It's covered with blue-flecked carpeting, slightly stained. The cleanest parts, she notices, bending to look, are under the seats, where humans don't go.

She straightens, lifts her head and looks straight into the eyes of Dave Trenton.

'Oh!' they both cry.

He smiles. 'Hello, Kate! I didn't know you lived down here.'

She nods, embarrassed. He is a manager, suited, sensible. He probably packs a lunchbox. And flosses.

'I don't,' she says. 'Well, I do, at weekends. My... my mother's house is in Henford, and my sister...' She can feel the old stutter about to play up. 'I... I live in Streatham during the week.'

'Oh, I see. I think your mother died recently?' She nods.

'I'm sorry,' he says. She nods again. He probably is. She rarely sees him at work. The theatre is a big place.

The train shudders, stops. They both watch the circular button, waiting. She has her hand near it, poised, just so he knows the situation is under control. The delay seems interminable. She can feel her cheeks flushing.

'Are you visiting someone in Eastleigh?'

'No, no, I—'

The beeping starts, and the button lights up. She jabs it. Nothing happens. She jabs it again. He reaches across and, gently moving her arm, presses the button firmly until the doors open. They both step out into fog. The rain has stopped. She glances at him. His eyes are kind.

'Kate, are you alright?'

'Yes. No!' she says, the cold air jerking her back to life. 'I had a special present made for my sister – she's in a home, severely disabled – and I left it on the train at Henford. I got on to look but I couldn't find it, and then the train left.' It hits her with sudden clarity. 'I need to ask the driver!' And she begins to run.

'Kate!' he calls but she keeps running. She is near the front, and she can see a woman hanging out of the driver's window.

'Excuse me! Excuse me. Can you help? I left something on the train at Henford and I can't find it. Would a cleaner have taken it? Could they have put it somewhere?'

'No cleaners, love, not at this time of night. Step back! That's right.' The woman leans back and adjusts something on her dashboard. The doors beep.

'I have to go. Gotta catch up. There's a Lost and Found at Oxted. You'll have to go there.'

The train begins to move. Kate walks with it, still talking. 'But that's miles away. Can I ring them? How will I...?'

The platform, with its lights and benches, slopes away. Beyond, there is nothing, just a gathering fog, darkness. The driver puts her head out of the window before the fog swallows the train completely.

'Oxted!' she shouts. The word echoes across the concrete towards her: 'O–X–T–E–D–D–D–D!'

Kate stops, teeters on the edge, regains her balance. At her side, Dave Trenton appears. They both stand there, out of breath, watching the train's tail lights fade.

After a while, Kate says, 'She said...'

'I heard.' He puts down his briefcase. 'Look, I can't take you to Oxted. It's too far in this fog. You could go tomorrow on the train? But I'll take you to Henford, if you like.'

She frowns. 'Why were you on that train?'

'Long story. I live in Eastleigh. My car's in the garage. It wasn't ready after work, so I thought I'd visit my aunt in Henford. But I'm in no hurry to get home. I'll take you.'

She considers this. He is the head of HR and wears shiny shoes. His eyes crinkle when he smiles. His briefcase is ageing and made of brown leather. Also, he is old, even older than she is. All these things combine to convince her, in an instant, that he's probably not an axe murderer. Hope takes her by the hand.

'It will be OK,' he tells Kate, smiling.

'Do you think so?'

'Of course!'

The weight of the day fidgets, settles. Hope sits with her, whispers in her ear. It is nearly done. Dave will take her to Henford. On the way to the home, she will buy chocolate for Megan. She will hug her and apologise, telling her the present is on its way. Megan will scream and cry and Pat will help to calm her down and she will produce the chocolate and Megan's eyes will light up. She'll train it to Oxted tomorrow. If it's not there, she has three days until Christmas. She'll think of something.

She exhales. Her breath curls in the fog damply. 'Thank you,' she tells him. 'That's very kind.'

The garage is close by and the car is ready. They don't talk much on the journey: he hunching to see the fog-laden lanes, she trying not to feel anxious. The air is thick with unknowing. The car grinds and halts in the twisty roads as other vehicles appear and they pull in. After what seems like hours, they reach the main road.

Dave rocks back, clearly relieved as the fog thins. Streetlights give a shout of welcome. A perfect cone of light falls from each one. The atmosphere loosens, swims.

'What are you doing for Christmas?'

She has answered this question so many times, it's automatic. It satisfies people. She only winces a second after, remembering he knows too much. 'I am going to visit my sister.'

The silence yawns, stretches. A sign looms whitely ahead. *Welcome to HENFORD*. And underneath, *Twinned with Poules sur Terre*.

'What about you?' She braces herself for visiting relatives, children.

'I'm going to visit my aunt.'

He turns his head, and their eyes meet in a moment of perfect understanding.

He stops for her on the high street but insists on waiting while she nips into a tinsel-covered Waitrose to buy chocolate. When he finally pulls up outside The Heights, she can see Megan at the window, silhouetted, waiting. Her heart sinks. Guilt pokes her in the ribs.

'If you'd been more careful, this would not have happened. Who leaves things like that on the train?'

She closes her ears to Guilt's accusing voice, turns to grab her rucksack, gets out.

She leans down into the open door.

'Thank you,' she says.

'You're welcome!' says Dave Trenton. He really does have the nicest eyes.

'Happy Christmas. I hope it goes alright... with your aunt,' she ventures.

'It'll be fine.' He gives a determined smile. 'She's old and a bit odd, but lovely. There'll be others there too, though you never know quite who. Good luck with the present!'

'Thank you.'

There is no one at reception so she goes straight to Megan's room. But when she opens the door, she gasps. There is a sea of Christmas paper and, as Megan turns, Kate sees the teddy being hugged to death in her arms. Megan reaches out to Kate, her face alight. Kate leans down to hug her sister, whose joy is as bright as the silver paper around her.

Pat is behind them, holding a tray.

'Kate!' she says. 'I'm so sorry. I was going to hide it but she was with me when it arrived, and once she saw it was a Christmas present, well, you know what she's like!'

The room is stifling. Kate shucks off her bag and jacket. She stares at the teddy, bewildered.

'But how...?'

Pat laughs. 'My grandson was on the train and heard someone leaving a message for me, something about having a present for Megan and the train being late.'

She puts the tray down, begins to fold washing. 'Stupid boy left his rucksack on the train...'

She seems to realise what she's said. 'Oh Kate, I'm sorry, I didn't mean—'

'It's fine. I was stupid too.'

'Well, he rushed back to get it and saw this in the luggage rack. It was roughly where he heard the voice, so he thought he'd drop it off when he cycled past.'

Kate remembers now. She put it up in the rack. She never does that. Then she remembers the boy, the bulging rucksack.

'That's incredible!' she says. 'What are the odds? Please thank him so much!'

Relief blossoms in her chest. Dazed by her good fortune, she leans down and picks up some wrapping paper, the bit with the label. She reads her own writing.

To my dearest Megan,
Happy Christmas!
With all my love, Mumma xx

'Mumma!' shouts Megan. She lifts the teddy in the air. 'Mumma!' she crows.

And there she is, their mother, in the patchwork memories that make up the bear. One arm is her flowered blouse, the other her Sunday dress. Her favourite apron smooths its brow. Her old knitting bag hugs its tummy.

'So clever,' says Pat, admiring it.

Kate smiles. She's so grateful it's been found. She'd had to be pretty inventive when Megan kept asking for Mumma for Christmas.

*

Later, on the way home, she passes the station. There is a light rain. Despair is waiting on the bench with the London *Metro*. Its eyes bore holes in her back.

It still sounds weird to treat her emotions as if they were people, but it was the last thing Esther, her counsellor, said to her before she went on sick leave. *Try it, Kate. It can help.* It does.

She turns back towards Despair. 'Go!' she says. 'There's no place for you here.'

Despair glowers. Kate keeps walking towards the crossing. She thinks of Christmas, their first one without Mum. Moments of despair are inevitable, but for her, for Megan, this is not the end of the line. She waits for the lights, does not look back at Despair.

If she had, she would have seen it fading, like print on wet paper.

Christmas at the Masala Ram

'Madam, it will be no problem for me, no problem at all. We can bring it. My son will bring it.'

Sunil raises his head from the bar and glares in the general direction of his father. What in God's name is the old man promising now? It sounds as though he's agreeing to deliver a takeaway outside the delivery zone. Again. Honestly, he has no idea how to run a modern business. *No... i... dea.*

Ram replaces the phone in its cradle. Much to his son's irritation, he insists on keeping the antique brass telephones, the sort he probably used at home. In India.

'It's a nice touch!' he had explained, when Sunil pointed out they didn't need them any more. 'It reminds people of the old ways. It is the *retro* look!'

Sunil had put his head in his hands. He knew his dad would have heard this expression somewhere, in the street or on TV. What he couldn't bring himself to say, seeing the light dim in the old man's eyes, was that this definitely was *not* what people meant by retro.

'Son...' Ram is wandering across the restaurant nodding and smiling at the regulars. 'A word, please?'

But before he reaches Sunil, Tiffany appears from the other side of the swing door. She slams a plastic bag straining with takeaway dishes onto the counter.

'COLLINS!' she bellows, as if to a wayward student.

'Ahhh, Mr Collins!' Ram turns to smile at one of their long-standing customers. He is rubbing his hands together with delight. Sunil winces.

'How good it is to see you again. I hope Mrs Collins is well? And the family?'

Mr Collins (Guy, as everyone calls him apart from Sunil's father) smiles and jerks his head at Tiffany's disappearing butt. 'She doesn't warm up, does she?' He winks.

Sunil agrees. Tiffany is a pain and should go, along with the telephones and Ram's obsequious behaviour.

'Ahhh, dear Tiff,' says Ram. Sunil winces again. 'She is doing so well. You know she has special needs. Very special...' He shakes his head sadly. Sunil's head is lowered over the bar, practically touching the bar towel.

'I take her to help my friend, her father, and to do my bit for our community.' Sunil is working hard not to mouth the next part. 'You know, after the partition, it was hard for all of us. We had to leave the country we loved. But we have made a life here and we are part of this country now.'

Ram finishes with his customary sideways shake of the head, eyes brimming with emotion. Sunil cannot look. *Part of what country?* he wants to shout. *Oh, you mean the country that allowed racism to flourish in schools, so I got beaten up by kids and put down by teachers? You mean the country that made it twice as hard for me to get interviews because of my surname? Yeah sure, great to be here...*

But once, when he was trying to have this out with his father, Papa-ji had risen up with such righteous indignation that Sunil worried he might have a heart attack. Ram had claimed, loudly, that this racism happened years ago, and the government wasn't responsible for how individuals behaved, that they had to move on. Anyway, he had concluded, wiping his brow with a hankie the size of a towel, this prejudice wasn't an issue for the grandchildren.

Sunil had somehow restrained himself from shouting that it was absolutely an issue for the grandchildren. Amira still faces it in her twenties, in the city. As for Raza, still at uni, his being passed over for placements could only be accounted for in one way. He had achieved outstanding results and even the Placement Officer had been unable to hide her surprise. In the end, with Sunil's help, he had managed to secure a part-time role, shadowing a relative of one of the Masala Ram's best customers. Unfortunately, this had strengthened his father's belief in the kindness of 'this great country'.

Ram only ever sees the good in things, and quite frankly, after a lifetime of bigotry and prejudice, Sunil wonders how he can continue to pretend to himself so convincingly.

Guy picks up his takeaway, and nods at Sunil.

'Thanks,' he says. 'Happy Christmas.'

'We don't celebrate Christmas.' Sunil knows his smile is grudging, tight. But Guy should know. They should all know this.

Guy has the grace to look embarrassed. 'Oh yeah, 'course. Sorry. Happy New Year, then!'

Sunil rolls his eyes at the man's back while Ram rushes forward to open the door. He stumbles and the door, surprised, swings open with a grunt. A whiff of snow and woodsmoke charms its way into the room. Sunil hates to admit it, but he loves the smells of a dying year – pine and cinnamon and roasting chestnuts from the stall on the corner.

His father closes the door and turns. *Here we go.*

'You are *so* rude!' Ram hisses in Punjabi, tottering towards him, adjusting the ridiculous white serviette he insists on laying over his arm. 'You *know* Christmas is our best time of year, but you *insist* on sabotaging our business.' Sunil opens his mouth to

35

protest but his father is on a roll. '*Why* do you not care about *everything* I built here? Why do you not want to *help* me?' He swings his arm dramatically round in a semi-circle, taking in the waiting customers, the delivery boys, the marble steps, at the top of which are glimpses of seated diners and tinsel.

'I am *not* trying to sabotage you, Papa-ji,' he growls back. He cannot help himself. He is so tired, so frustrated. 'But this business will not survive if we don't change! We need to modernise, try something new. We cannot pretend things are still the same as when you first came here.' The back of his neck feels hot. He scratches it absently. Tiffany appears.

'ROBERTS!' she yells with an accompanying thump. The two bags of food are slammed onto the counter with vigour. There is a dribble of masala sauce through plastic.

Sunil lets his father do his bit with the Roberts order while he hisses at Tiffany. '*Please* can you sound a bit nicer when you bring the orders out? And be careful!'

She stares at him briefly. 'O-*KAY!*' she shouts. Sunil can feel the veins in his neck fattening like slugs. He loosens his collar.

'All you can think of is making money!' His father is off again, standing close to the bar, watching him draw a pint for a customer. 'If I could see you just trying to *give* to this community, I might be willing to listen to your ideas, son. But all you do is take. Take, take, take.'

Sunil hands the pint to the customer and accepts the money. Sweat is pricking his scalp like drawing pins. The atmosphere of the Masala Ram, with its antique wall lights and heavy wallpaper, is suddenly suffocating. His breathing begins to quicken. He tugs at his collar again, loosens his tie.

'Where's that delivery to?' he asks, remembering the phone call.

Ram is taken aback, clearly expecting conflict about this. *And who can blame him*, thinks Sunil. There always has been in the past. The delivery area was key to maintaining profit margins, and Ram's kindness constantly threatens these. Ram rubs his eyes. In spite of his irritation, Sunil sees how tired he is. The circles under those eyes have deepened recently, and he wouldn't have thought that was even possible.

'Lady Trenton,' Ram replies. There is a defensive look in his eyes. 'Her butler, you know... he is away.'

Sunil has to work hard at keeping his temper. Ashdown House is six miles away, in the forest. Its butler, the only remaining live-in help for the old lady, is nice enough but insists on parking the Daimler on the double yellow lines by the door of the restaurant. It is dark and cold and there is snow on the way. They have never delivered to her before. Sunil is trying to decide whether to object or just go with it for the sake of escaping, when Tiffany barrels back through the swing door, her face red and blotchy with kitchen heat.

'TRENTON!' she bawls, but seeing Sunil's face, she manages to adeptly slow the last part of the carrier bag's journey to the counter, so after its breakneck whizz through the air, it lands with a whisper, right in front of him.

There is a silence. Even the waiting takeawayers look impressed. One of them gives a small cheer. Sunil glowers at Tiffany. Then he grabs the bag and storms out of the restaurant.

The forest road is steep and dark. Flakes of snow have begun a half-hearted descent and there's black ice. Sunil leans forward in the driver's seat and adjusts the headlights. The beam, long and low, picks out fallen branches crisp with cold, and the odd deer. You have to watch out for them in the forest. Last winter someone swerved to miss one and drove into a tree. He did not survive. Sunil does not like the word *died* and refuses to use it. There is something so final about it, so stark. Unless you ask, it gives you nothing. *Did not survive* is kinder.

He sighs. Nothing will change at the Masala Ram unless he changes it. To be fair, he has tried, but always faltered at some point along the way. Since his mother's death, his father's hold over the business has seemed weaker, frailer. He has always blazed with anger every time Sunil mentions the changes he wants to make, but now his hands shake too. He still retains control of the bank account but seems less confident about sales figures, worries he might miss something. Occasionally he asks Sunil for help instead of proudly managing alone.

A memory: coming here with his parents as a boy. On days off, they'd bring a picnic to the forest, find a clearing, throw down a rug. While his mother arranged endless Tupperware boxes of food for tea, he and his father would play hide and seek or football. Ram was a different man in those days. There was light in his eyes.

The road curves suddenly and Sunil brakes too hard, the car skidding and jolting on the hidden ice. It spins and turns, cutting out as it comes to a halt on the verge near a ditch. Sunil's heart is racing. This is not the peace-filled break he had planned, away from the restaurant. The snow is thickening, the heater has stopped working and the silence around him is fat with menace.

'Don't be a fool,' he pants aloud. 'Just slow down!'

He starts the engine and, reversing slowly, inches carefully back onto the narrow road, his father's voice echoing in his ears. *Your car is your friend. Don't treat it like an enemy! If you pound it to death, it will be the death of you!* He found himself saying this to Raza last year while sitting, terrified, in the passenger seat just after Raza passed his test. The memory makes him shiver. He is turning into his father.

Will Amira and Raza roll their eyes at him one day, at his advice, his intransigence? In his own mind, he is a progressive compared to his father, free of cliché, forward-thinking, with so many ideas for changes to the business, so many plans. But if Raza ever throws in accountancy and comes back to run the restaurant, will he, Sunil, have ripened into a version of Ram? More memories: he and Amira arguing over short skirts; lecturing Raza about his drunken Freshers' Week. He thinks of their quiet defiance, the size and shape of it, an almost physical presence grown large between them. He pushes the thought aside.

The snow is settling. Everything slows – the wipers, the car, his beating heart. There's a dream-like feel to the road and the trees, idling under their crystal covers. Google Maps has stopped working. There's probably no signal out here, but he thinks he knows roughly where he's going. He's deep in the forest now, and the trees themselves direct him. One points ahead and to the right – a gust of wind? A branch bends and hisses *Happy Christmas* – a fall of snow?

'We don't celebrate Christmas!' he tells the trees. They quiver with mirth and throw fists of snow which punch the car with heavy sighs.

Finally, there they are, a couple of old-fashioned lamps, not unlike the ones at the restaurant, either side of a huge iron gateway. The one the butler had told them about, an open mouth in a fascia of twisted branches. Sunil brakes gently and eases the car into the drive, which is, strangely, wider than the road.

'Crikey!' He looks around as he putters up a gradual incline. Flanking the drive, there is open ground. As the road twists and turns, the headlights pick out a glint of settled snow. Astonishingly, the trees seem to have withdrawn, although they surge back as he crests the hill and turns a corner. The driveway is long and wide and very dark.

Eventually he sees one or two lights wink between branches. He rounds a corner, crunches over gravel and pulls up in front of the house. His jaw, cold and clenched from the stress of the journey, falls open.

He gets out of the car, lifting his eyes to the immense building before him. There are only a couple of lights, in the porch and either side of the circular turning area. But he can see rows of windows, a massive door and, further up, the outline of a tower, barely visible in the falling snow.

As he stands there gawping, the oak door swings open and two figures emerge: one an older lady, tall and dressed in a thick skirt and jumper, the other a young, bearded man with a cello. The sight is so surprising, so unusual – two such different people in such a remote place, she in her red skirt, he shouldering a cello and rucksack – that Sunil stares.

'You must be Sunil,' the woman says. 'Pleased to meet you.' She walks right up to him and extends her hand. Despite her cut-glass accent, she is polite. 'I've heard so much about you,' she adds.

Sunil frowns. How could this be? He glances from the woman to the man, who just stands there, passive, his dark eyes watching, snow on his beard.

'I... Lady Trenton? There's only a takeaway for one,' Sunil says.

'That's right,' she says, 'Jem is just leaving.' Sunil reaches into the car for the bag containing the food. He looks around as he passes it to her. There is no other vehicle in sight.

'I hope it's not cold,' he tells her.

She smiles. 'No problem,' she says. 'I know how to use a microwave!' She holds the takeaway close to her body, like a hot-water bottle. Her hair, a loose knot on top of her head, is now dotted with snow.

Sunil nods and makes as if to get into the car.

'You don't mind, do you?' Lady Trenton motions towards the man. 'He needs to get to Henford, and he doesn't have a car.'

Unbelievable, thinks Sunil. And then, *The cheek of it!* He looks at the man, who looks back at him in silence. Not pleading, not even hopeful; impassive, as though he is used to provoking outrage and has learned not to care.

Meanwhile Lady Trenton stands there, secure in her white upper-class assumption that everyone will do her bidding. He, Sunil, has driven through a snowstorm to bring her a takeaway (for one) and diced with death while skidding on ice. But instead of thanking him, the woman is effectively ordering him to give a lift to some stranger.

'Actually, I do mind.'

He says this, while drawing himself up to his full height. His snow-flecked hair, he later imagines, gives him that sense of dignity, the gravitas needed with this pompous woman.

But that's the problem: it's all imagined. And he doesn't say he minds, although he does. Instead, he looks uncertainly from one to the other.

'Look, it's fine,' says Lady Trenton. 'He's fine. He's been doing some jobs for me, earned himself bed and board. But he's playing tonight in Henford, and I couldn't think of a way of getting him there.'

Sunil rubs his hands together and kicks snow from the edge of the car. Did the woman order a takeaway (for one) just to get her handyman a lift? Surely not! Has she not heard of taxis? Though, to be fair, the Henford taxis are a bit random, depending on fires and funerals. Of the brothers who run it, one is a fireman, the other a pallbearer. His daughter still talks of her embarrassment at being driven home from the station in an empty hearse.

The man called Jem steps forward. 'You'd be doing me a favour,' he says. 'I'm playing at The Star, you know; carols and the like.' He wraps his arms tenderly around the cello case.

Sunil considers. The man's voice is gentle, his expression polite. Jem glances warily at the woman, who nods at him encouragingly.

Sunil thinks it must be her idea. He feels cross, forced into a corner, obliged. But the guy looks harmless enough. Sunil sighs.

'Get in,' he says. 'The cold must be bad for your instrument.' He gets back into the car, thinking of how his son would wind him up about this last comment. As he slams the door, a ribbon of snow bolts from the window to the ground. Jem lays his cello reverently on the back seat along with his rucksack and then slides in beside him. Sunil starts the engine. Lady Trenton taps on the window, which he opens an inch.

'Thank you,' she says with as much feeling as someone like her can. 'And don't worry about your father. Just give him time.'

'Sorry?' Sunil winds the window down another notch. What on earth is she talking about?

Lady Trenton brings her mouth closer to the opening. Her eyes are very blue; there is lipstick on her teeth.

'He needs time, to adapt to the idea of change,' she says crisply. 'He lost so much, you know, in India.'

Sunil stares. 'What do you—' But she turns on her heel and marches back towards the huge door, arms folded tight around the carrier bag containing the takeaway.

'Happy Christmas!' she calls.

Sunil grunts. 'I don't celebrate Christmas,' he mumbles.

There is no more to be said. He reverses the car, which slides reluctantly on the snowy ground. Eventually the revs are high enough to begin the slippery descent to the main road. It's snowing so hard that the windscreen can't be cleared; the wipers merely lever clumps of it from side to side. Sunil leans forward, gripping the steering wheel, which he jams into his chest. In the mirror, the snow gradually obscures the woman and her red skirt standing under the light by the door. She grows smaller and smaller, a red dot on white paper. Why doesn't she go inside? Sunil sees that Jem is watching the wing mirror. There is some history there.

He reaches the end of the drive with relief and swings onto the road. Here, the snow has parted into the rut-shaped furrows ploughed by other cars. They drive for a while in silence. Sunil needs to concentrate. Jem appears to acknowledge this.

When they reach the edge of the forest and the roundabout near the by-pass, Sunil unclenches his hands and sighs. He glances at Jem. 'So, do you often play in pubs?'

His passenger appears to consider the question before answering.

'Not often,' he says. 'But at this time of year it's a good way to make money. And I enjoy it.' He returns Sunil's glance. 'Do you enjoy your job?'

This is unexpected, and annoying. Because Sunil doesn't. It seems to be one long battle with his father these days. He, Sunil, wants to modernise. His father likes things the way they are. In Sunil's view, Ram wastes money, gives too much away, bangs on about the community, about doing their bit. Sunil thinks with irritation of Lady Trenton's comment about what Ram had lost when he fled India. How come she knows about that when he doesn't? His father never talks about it. And it's clearly painful, so he doesn't ask.

But he doesn't want to explain this to Jem, so he says, 'It's alright.'

Jem nods. They continue for a while in silence. Sunil sighs.

'I want things to change,' he tells Jem, 'and my father doesn't.'

Jem nods again. 'What kind of change?'

They reach the edge of the town. Streetlights march towards them. Sunil has that rare desire to confide.

'Just, you know, be imaginative. We were the first Indian in Henford. Now there are seven! We could set up a cocktail bar, do up the garden, start a catering service. Why not?'

Jem considers, stroking his beard. 'Maybe your dad's happy the way things are. He has a decent life, a business, a family. Maybe that's enough.'

Sunil slows for the twenty-mile-per-hour speed limit. Light spills from shop windows decked for Christmas. A group of youths are messing about on the pavement. One is posting snowballs into a postbox. Above the road, the town is strung with coloured lights. A Christmas tree shimmers near the green. He wonders why, of all the places in the UK they could have gone to after escaping the horrors of Partition, his parents chose this one. He has never asked.

Sunil brakes as they approach the Tudor watering house, its windows decked with stars.

'And you?' he asks Jem. 'Are you content?'

His passenger looks up at The Star and opens the car door, but doesn't move. Sunil shivers as cold air swims in.

'Yes,' he says, 'I am. I don't need much, to be honest. I'll earn enough tonight for a meal and a place to kip.' He indicates the sleeping bag strapped under his rucksack.

'But what about tomorrow?' Sunil is curious. How can the man live like this?

Jem smiles. He swings long legs out of the car. 'Something always turns up,' he says. 'Like your dad, I've had worse.'

Sunil wants to ask him what was worse. What happened to him? Why doesn't he live and work in one place, like other people? Instead, he watches Jem open the back door and pull out his cello and rucksack. He shuts the back door, hitches the bag over his shoulder and bends down, his hand on the roof of the car.

'You and I,' he tells Sunil, 'we stand out in a town like this; we're different. But it's our town too.'

Sunil wishes he didn't have to go. He wants to continue talking to this curious stranger with his long hair and mild manner. He wants to ask him things. But instead, he checks Jem doesn't have to wait around in the cold, asks when he'll finish work. Jem thanks him and slams the door. Sunil lets out the brake and, careful of the icy road, drives off towards the restaurant.

Later, after he's checked the bookings, served drinks, cleared tables, Sunil slides gratefully into an empty chair opposite his father. Dishes of curry fill the top table. They call it this because it's in the bay window and from the other side, the chairs opposite Sunil, diners have the best view of the town. The high street drops away towards the green, lined with independent shops lit for Christmas. And on the other side it rises steeply towards the South Downs, the houses on either side of the road shouldered together like cats.

Sunil serves them both and asks questions. He wants to know, wants to find out what motivates the man, what makes him tick. Why did his parents never tell him what really happened to them at Partition? What finally drove them to leave their country for one so far away?

Ram holds himself still as Sunil tells him he has never felt able to ask. It was never mentioned, never discussed, a taboo subject. Why has Ram never told him of the circumstances that led him and his mother to leave India?

Ram slumps in his chair. He brings his hands from under the table and lays them, palms upward, on the snowy cloth. When he speaks, his voice is low and slow, somehow distant even though he's sitting across the table. He's staring not at Sunil but over his shoulder at the picture-perfect view of the town with its strings of lights and covering of snow. He tells his son slowly what happened. What strikes Sunil most is the way his face changes shape as he speaks, as if reliving past versions of itself. There is bitterness, brokenness, a barely suppressed rage. And he begins to understand why his parents never told him. Why would you relive atrocities like these? He cannot take his eyes from the old man's face.

What happened at Partition was a bloodbath. It reaches the point where Sunil wants him to stop, but this is his history too. It's only when his father's hands begin to shake that he covers them with his own.

'Enough.' His voice is gentle. He hesitates for a moment. 'Thank you,' he whispers.

After a bit, Ram's hands stop shaking. He moves them from under Sunil's and puts them back in his lap. He draws himself up, as if putting on another self. He looks at Sunil then.

'Son,' he says, 'I know you think I'm old-fashioned, risk-averse, but now you see why. I cannot...' His shoulders sag briefly before he draws himself up again and looks at Sunil fiercely. 'I cannot lose everything again.'

There is a pause. It's getting late. There's a clatter from the till as his cousin cashes up, from the kitchen the sound of a radio. In the bar, someone switches on a hoover.

'I met a man today,' says Sunil. 'He was at Lady Trenton's. I gave him a lift into town.'

Ram nods. As quickly as it came, the ferocity has gone. Sunil cannot make out this new expression in the old man's eyes. Could it be approval?

'He was a bit of a misfit, but I liked him,' he says. 'Told him to pop in sometime this week if he'd like a meal.'

Ram is nodding on repeat. 'Well done, son,' he says. 'It's right that we give what we can to this community. We're all part of it, even the misfits.'

They look at each other and smile. A wave of tiredness sweeps over Sunil. It's been a long day.

His father is watching him. He raises his glass.

'Go home, son. I'll lock up. But Christmas at the Masala Ram – your mother loved it. It's not our celebration but the community comes alive, and they bring their parties here.

Amira and Raza will be home, there'll be bank holidays. Let's make the most of it!'

He eases himself to his feet, picks up the glasses, touches his son on the shoulder.

There is light in his eyes.

The Photo

People think that blindness means darkness. Like when you turn the lights off or put the bins out at night. But blindness isn't dark. It's smeared writing you can't read, an out-of-focus photo, thumbprints on a lens. Blindness is light. But light can't always help you see.

Kim thinks this as she studies the bedroom mirror. Her reflection is formless, a void, a blurred picture; how she so often feels these days. As if the old Kim – friendly, warm, confident – has faded and no one, including herself, can see her any more. A descent into panic always hovers at the door: perhaps I won't find it/her/them because I won't be able to see. She opens her right eye and the bedroom swims back. *It'll be fine. One eye is enough. That's what they said: People cope with one eye.* But one eye isn't always enough when there's damage there too. She glances along the cornice at the top of the wall. Over on the right somewhere, it kinks. Only it doesn't. The lie is in her eye.

Outside, a gust of wind makes the window rattle. The weather outlook is bad but it's snug in the bedroom, the lamps casting circles of light that make her feel held. She wonders if Ralph has come up from the studio. Daisy is lying on the bed, watching her. Her daughter is warm, appraising.

'Mum, you look great. Honestly.'

She knows Daisy is honest. Her daughter wouldn't say anything she doesn't mean. If Kim was wearing something that looked wrong, she would tell her. When you work in a theatre, you have a good eye. You know what goes and what doesn't.

Kim turns sideways and smooths the velvet across her stomach. 'Bulge line?' she asks.

'Nope,' Daisy says. She whips herself into a sitting position and reaches out a hand, strokes the black and silver material.

'Mum, what are you scared of? You look gorgeous. You're going to see friends. You love London!'

'*Loved*,' Kim replies. She sinks onto the bed next to her daughter and they stretch out together, side to side, head to head, eye to eye.

'It's different now. I have much less confidence. I'm always worried I'll get lost or I won't find people or I'll go into the Gents. Make a fool of myself somehow.'

'Just be honest.' Daisy reaches across and pushes the fringe away from her mother's eyes. 'Tell them you've been ill. You're visually impaired now. You can struggle in new places, and they might have to be your white stick.'

Kim smiles. Daisy's earnest face makes her ever so slightly tearful. Where did this wise, funny, caring woman come from? How could she and Ralph have made her?

On cue, Ralph pokes his head around the door. 'All going well, girls? Only two hours to go. You'd better get a move on.' A chorus of protest; a pillow and a shoe box hit the door at speed, and he retreats. The box, which had contained the sparkly slingbacks Kim occasionally lifts a leg to admire, plummets to the floor. Ignoring it, she snuggles back onto her side, accidentally flipping the card insert from the tights packet. It shimmies onto the windowsill.

Moments like these are precious these days. She thinks of the funny little girl who spent her toddler years screaming with mirth or anger and stepping over things in strict rotation 'to be fair to my feet'. Now she is her friend and friends 'get you'. And when you're literally made from the same stuff, you understand each other completely.

Kim knows she's a bit fragile because of her eyes, and emotional because of the menopause, but she sometimes wakes in the morning to an almost physical pain because her children aren't there any more. After dreaming about them – often about their old, unbridled excitement at Christmas or another much-loved holiday – she pushes through the stupor of sleep to realise: it's over. They're adults with their own lives and have left her to hers. This is a good thing; of course it is. Unless she's feeling fragile or menopausal or has pitched some content to a company who've turned her down.

She doesn't understand. She's never been the kind of mum who has poured herself into kids and home to the exclusion of all else. She's always worked, always had interests. Even when she had three under five, she had fought to keep part of life for herself: paid for childcare, gone out with friends. So this onslaught of grief, the sense of loss, after they've been independent for so long, takes her by surprise. Perhaps it's just ageing; an awareness that time, that great leveller, is running out.

Daisy burrows into the duvet and puts one leg across Kim's, the way she used to.

'So, remind me again? There's Lucy…'

'She's the blonde one,' says Kim. She pulls the remaining pillow under her head and tips onto her back. 'Lucy's lovely but very pretty and thin still, so I sometimes feel a bit… lumpish.'

'Mother!'

'I know, I know. I shouldn't judge on weight, but there we are. Lucy works for a fashion house – Paul Smith, I think, though she may have moved on (she always does) – so probably feels she has to keep trim.'

Daisy pulls a face. 'Maybe. What about Rebecca? I thought she was the successful one?'

'Oh, they're all successful.' Kim sighs and closes her good eye. The ceiling looks much better like this. All the patches have gone, and the lightshade looks shabby chic, instead of just shabby. 'I always feel I've failed somehow, settling for life as a content writer.'

'You haven't settled!' Daisy frowns. 'Crikey, Mum, you've had a career, raised three kids, started your own business. Be proud of what you've achieved. Especially with me!' She flexes her arm and laughs, wagging her finger. 'Comparison is the thief of joy, remember!'

It occurs to Kim it should be the other way round – she doling out advice, Daisy taking it – but the shift had already begun before the inflammatory disease that stole her sight.

She opens her eye. 'I've always wanted to be a reporter,' she tells her daughter. 'Don't tell me it's not too late—'

'It's not too late…'

Kim ignores her. 'Anyway, Rebecca is a lawyer,' she continues. 'She's at a big firm in London and her husband works at the House of Commons. Her children are all prodigies—'

'Like us, then?' Daisy pokes her with her foot. They laugh. 'Show me photos.'

Kim picks up her phone and opens *Photos, Reunion*. She scrolls through to find last year's get-together, clicking on an image ripe with tinsel and red ribbon. And there they are, around a table in a restaurant – she, Rebecca, Lucy and Di.

She hands the phone to Daisy. Her daughter gives a low whistle.

'You all look gorgeous! Nowhere near your age. How do you do it?'

There's a spatter of rain on the window. The lamps flicker. Kim wonders if there'll be another power cut. As Daisy hands the phone back, she stares at the photo again and shivers. It was a year ago, before her health problems struck, and to her (admittedly damaged) eyes, in her red dress and high shoes she looks ten years younger. But it's more than that; she looks lighter. As though sadness, whose leaden weight sometimes stops her breathing, hasn't met her yet.

The reunion every Christmas since school is in its fortieth year: something to celebrate. Di has booked the Crown Club in Hackney, which Kim has never heard of but was assured is one of the best in the world. Number thirty-five to be exact (she googled it); surely not much of an accolade.

'This is the WORLD we're talking about,' Di insisted on the WhatsApp chat, followed by five exclamation marks and a globe emoji. So, they had given in, as they always did. But nobody minds because Di is lovely, has excellent taste and puts in the effort when the rest of them forget to.

Kim is both dreading and looking forward to it. Why hasn't she told them she's been ill? Because with people you grew up with, an unspoken question hangs in the air: *How am I doing, compared to you?* The curious alchemy of female friendship can make or break you, sometimes in the same evening.

Daisy rolls off the bed and Kim sits up.

'I'm going to enjoy it,' she says, stretching her hands and admiring the nails. 'I'm not going to overthink, and I'll try not to feel wobbly. It's a lovely reunion with old friends. Like you say, if it comes to it, I'll tell them.' Ignoring her daughter's cynical look, she nods with satisfaction.

The weather is awful, so Daisy drives her to the station. Kim is glad because the train is late, and Ralph is in the very last stages of a commissioned painting which is doing his head in. It was hard to persuade him not to take her himself, but he could see the sense in it. She is relieved, as he would have insisted on waiting with her yet also itched to get back.

They sit in the car while it rocks in the wind, all steamed up and cosy. Kim rubs at the windscreen so they can see the automatic board announcing that the train will be twenty minutes late. The window display in the chemist this year is disappointing. But if you peer closely through a patch of windscreen, you can see a couple of battery-operated candles set in tinsel. A Santa-shaped water bottle and a rotating toothbrush look vile in the sickly glow.

A gust of wind flings a low branch at the car, making them jump. The dispassionate tones of an announcement snake along the platform towards them.

'*Platform one. The 18.23 to London Victoria is approximately twenty minutes late. We apologise for the inconvenience.*'

Kim tightens the belt on her coat. It's her for-best green velvet with a fake fur collar that makes her feel good. She rarely wears anything but jeans these days and relishes this once-a-year chance to dress up. She and Daisy chat about her daughter's plans – her job, her house – until the time has passed and Kim checks her reflection, pulls up her hood, kisses her daughter.

'I'm not going to tell you to be careful, Mum,' says Daisy, 'but you know where I am if you need me.'

'Don't be late!' she adds just before her mother slams the door.

Kim clatters onto the platform, grateful for the long coat, and marvels at how quickly times change.

The train is packed. Parents and kids jostle with theatregoers and a group of loutish types in the space by the door, who are loudly admiring each other's fancy dress. Kim is always sur-prised how popular costume parties are. Perhaps it's the chance to be someone else for a while. Now, that she can understand. She sits in a place for four. Next to her, by the window, is a priest in a leather jacket, who might or might not be one of the partygoers. Opposite are a woman reading a book and a man in dark glasses with a rucksack. The man looks uncomfortable, glancing round as though hoping to see someone. It occurs to her he could be a terrorist. *Do others have these thoughts?*

To distract herself, she looks out of the window, but they're in a tunnel and all she can see in the foreground is her own face. She tries to read the backwards writing of adverts on the opposite wall, then looks down and counts the floor tiles. As they bolt out of the tunnel, she abandons this and stares at lighted houses and industrial units, which flee past at dizzying speed. When the train slows to cross a bridge, she sees a high street below them. Wet windows glisten under threads of Christmas lights. She wonders which town it is. In the dark, she's lost her sense of direction.

The man in dark glasses gets up and pushes his way towards the next carriage. The woman with the book yawns and adjusts her headscarf. Someone dressed as a Christmas tree is describing how he got his branches wedged in a urinal at Brighton. His friends snort raucously. The train swings in the wind. *We are constantly reaffirming our place in the world*, Kim thinks, *making people laugh, or getting things done or being useful.*

Later, she will wonder how many other people have been plunged into darkness on a train screaming to a halt. She's sneaking a glance at the priest at the time, trying to work out if he's fake. She's leaning slightly towards him, and the force of the brakes combined with the wind makes the train tip so she's thrown across his seat. There's a collective gasp and a lot of swearing, though not from the priest. He must be the real deal. There is an acrid smell of brake fluid as the train slows. It seems to go on forever. At last, as the train levels out and grinds to a stop, she levers herself away with a mumbled apology. There is a moment of collective relief before shouting starts in the next carriage.

Kim has never moved so fast. As cries and loudly offered advice fill the air, she pushes her bag strap over her head, tips onto her hands and knees and fast-crawls towards the door. It's dark but there are a few phone torches on, enabling her to push between the people still standing – though most fell during the abrupt stop. She doesn't need her eyes anyway. She makes for the left-hand doors, which are two seats behind. Standing quickly, she fumbles up high for the emergency door panel. Finding it, she whips off a shoe and smashes it blindly with the heel.

'What the...?' Someone is at her side, flashing a torch in her eyes. She pushes him away. She pulls the handle and the doors open.

The wind and rain slam into her, taking her breath away. She clings to the edge of the open doors, shoes in hand, ready to jump. Behind her, there is chaos. Some people seem to be pushing towards the other carriage, away from the screams. Others lunge towards the exit doors as well. A couple of torches point towards the ground outside, revealing overgrown grass and a ditch. No one jumps. It is pitch black and they are seemingly in the middle of nowhere. It's a long way down.

Only now is she aware of her thudding heart, her dry mouth. Now that escape is in sight, she's afraid. It's a long way to jump and it's blisteringly cold. People are shouting all around her.

'Should we jump?'

'Jump, for God's sake!'

The torch weaving back and forth behind her settles briefly on the person alongside. It's the priest.

'Hold my hand,' he says. 'We'll jump together. After three. OK?'

She hesitates, her breathing fast and sore. Her hands are too sweaty. She wipes them on her coat and tries to see his face. It's mostly in shadow but his eyes are earnest.

A voice behind her (the person with the torch?) is impatient. 'For God's sake, jump! Or get out the way so we can!'

She's panting now. She grasps the priest's hand and looks out into the dark. The wind whips at her hair. At the side of the track are smudged outlines of trees and behind them, pockets of light from houses. She tries to focus on them and on the task in hand, but random memories compete for attention, chasing resolve away: Daisy's fat legs, Jem's curls, Tom's tantrums, Di's laugh – uproarious, free.

She's still holding her shoes in the other hand. She can't decide whether to put them on or not. The priest starts to count.

He gets to two and she's about to push herself to jump when the lights burst back on. The intercom crackles to life: *'This is a passenger announcement. This is a passenger announcement. Do not leave the train. Repeat: do not leave the train. There's been an incident on the track and an emergency stop. The police are on the way. All passengers should remain on the train. Repeat: remain on the train.'*

There's a brief silence. Then the clamour starts. People pick themselves up, start processing what's happened, release the stress.

'I thought I was a goner there!' shouts a woman dressed as a bauble.

'When you fell on me, I thought I was the goner!' says the Christmas tree, plumping his branches. They both shriek with laughter and relief.

Behind him, a man checks on an old lady, a mum comforts her child.

Kim is still holding the priest's hand. They are both shaking. She lets go. He is older than she thought, with creased eyes and greying temples.

'Thank God,' he says. 'Not a bomb. Probably a suicide attempt.' He realises what he's said. 'I mean—'

'*This is a passenger announcement. This is a passenger announcement.*' Voices fall quiet. '*The doors are about to close. Please move away from the doors. The doors are about to close.*'

Kim supposes others have broken the glass too. She shimmies away from the exit on her backside, dirtying her best coat. The doors beep and she uses the rail to pull herself to her feet. The carriage is full of sound and the smell of sweat.

She makes her way back to her seat as others have done. Even short-lived familiarity is safe. Like your holiday home on day two.

The priest follows her, his last words hovering in the air between them. They have to step over a couple of fallen cases and the people trying to retrieve them. She steps aside for him to move into his window seat, which he automatically does. The woman with the book is already in her seat opposite, texting. As soon as they sit, the priest turns to Kim.

'I'm Aidan,' he says. 'Are you OK? You looked deathly pale back there. I thought we would jump.'

She fumbles for a tissue, wipes the sweat from her face. 'Me too,' she says. She hesitates. 'I'm Kim, Kim Franklin. I'm fine.'

He leans a little closer, drops his voice. 'I feel so bad about what I said.' He swallows. 'About the suicide, if that's what it was...' He breaks off and wipes his own face with a leather sleeve.

'It's alright,' she says. She glances over towards the carriage where the screaming was. People are gathering around someone near the door.

'It's OK,' she tells him, 'we all say things like that when we're stressed. We don't mean them.'

He looks stricken. 'But it was a terrible thing to say. A suicide is the worst! It's just that one of my sisters has had a baby. She's waited so long. I'm on my way to see them and I couldn't bear it if...' He looks down. She sees the stubble above his dog collar, the loose skin at his neck.

Kim puts her hand on his arm. 'Forget it. It's fine,' she says. 'We've all had a shock. You didn't mean it that way.' She pats his arm as though giving absolution (*shouldn't it be the other way round?*).

He nods but still looks miserable. He whips out his phone and starts to message furiously. Kim can't help seeing the words *Hi Amy* and *I'm OK*. He looks up and she turns away.

'My twin,' he tells her. 'We always know when the other's in trouble. When she had a car crash the other day, I was beside myself. I couldn't get hold of her. I'm letting her know all is well.'

'Of course,' she replies guiltily. 'I didn't mean to pry.'

The woman with the book lifts her eyes from her phone. It's the first time they have seen her face.

'It wasn't suicide,' she says. 'It says here it was teenage dares on the track. Someone tripped and fell but he was spotted, and the signaller messaged the guard.' She is beautiful, with amber eyes held in perfect curves of liquid liner.

A train official is talking to the fancy-dress group. They're clustering around him asking how long they'll have to wait. Someone shouts in French on his phone. A baby cries.

The woman opposite is clearly waiting for her to say something. But Kim is mesmerised by her eyes. The man in dark glasses and the rucksack emerges from the cluster of people at the end of the aisle. He folds himself into his seat. Kim tries not to stare at him. It sounds awful, but she had thought at first it was him. A terrorist on a train. It wouldn't be the first time.

'I'm Maryam,' the woman tells her. 'I'm on the way to see my mother. She is old and worries a lot. So I don't think I will tell her about this.'

'I'm Kim. Oh, I don't blame you,' she says. 'She might imagine it worse than it was.' She hesitates. 'Although, to be fair, it was quite bad.'

Maryam shrugs. She looks straight at her. 'How did you open the doors so quickly?'

Kim clears her throat. 'I... I'm visually impaired,' she tells her, 'so I always check out new places. You know, to see where I am in relation to things – the toilets, the exit, other people. It makes me feel safe.'

Maryam's face is impassive, but she nods. 'That makes sense,' she says. And then she adds, as people do, 'You'd never know.'

The man in dark glasses hugs his rucksack tightly. 'Serious problems in people's eyes are at the back, in the retina,' he says blandly. 'You can't see them. I'm severely sight-impaired – blind – but no one would know.'

For a moment it looks as though he's about to take off his glasses. The moment passes. There is a breath. Kim is filled with guilt. Not a terrorist, a blind person.

'But you don't have a stick!' she blurts out. He laughs. It changes his face completely.

'I do have a stick, in my rucksack. A folded one. But I don't need it on this train. I take the same one to work every day and know it well. And I can see enough – shapes, lights – to get by. I wear dark glasses because they make me feel safe.' He smiles at her.

The train jolts and begins to move. There is a cheer. The two baubles start singing. Behind them, a child shouts, 'Go, train!'

'I'm so sorry,' Kim tells the blind man. But she can't tell what she's apologising for.

He gives a low laugh. 'What for?'

Maryam is flushed. She turns to him but looks at Kim. 'No, I am sorry,' she says. 'It was my ignorance. If I'd thought about it for a moment, I would have known that. I apologise.'

'Don't worry!' says the man. He fishes in his pocket and brings out a huge bar of chocolate. He rips it open with a practised hand.

'Have some!' he says, waving it. They do.

Aidan swallows a mouthful and looks towards Kim. 'We all react without thinking at times,' he says, 'particularly under stress. Isn't that right, Kim?'

Suddenly she can breathe again. She nods. 'Too right, Aidan,' she says. She looks across at him and smiles. There is something sticking out of his jacket pocket. It's a small gift, badly wrapped. The paper is covered in storks.

The train slows to a hum and slides into Victoria. They are thanked for travelling, wished a pleasant onward journey, reminded about belongings. As if everything has been normal, expected. But what's the alternative? *This service is approximately sixty minutes late due to lads on the line. We apologise for any inconvenience.*

It feels as though there should be an acknowledgement that this has been different to the journey they were expecting. But they're told to carry on, mind the gap, remember bags and children.

Kim has texted Ralph, Daisy and the girls, who all replied with appropriate levels of concern and outrage. She has ordered her food.

As she and her seatmates are getting up, the Christmas tree, untangling his branches from other passengers, waits for the blind man to move into the aisle. Then he puts his arm round him.

'Mate, it's been a pleasure!' he says, beaming. 'This guy is the one who told me not to ditch the cossie,' he tells them. 'And he can't even see it!'

The blind man swings the rucksack over his shoulder. 'Well, you rescued me from the loo,' he says. 'It was the least I could do!'

Kim pulls her coat around her, checks she has everything. As they inch towards the door, one of the baubles claps the man on the shoulder.

'We were impressed 'bout that, though,' he says. 'It's hard enough to aim on a train when you *can* see what you're doing!'

They all crow with laughter then. They get off the train and make their way along the platform, the blind man tapping his stick. There's a sense of relief, togetherness.

Kim feels warm towards the fancy-dress people, for looking after the blind man, for being upbeat, funny.

'Where's your party?' she asks them.

The Christmas tree goes through the wide exit on account of his girth. He and Kim stand together on the other side of the barrier with the blind man, Maryam and Aidan. Maryam is watching them curiously. Aidan is texting.

'Charing Cross,' says the other bauble. Her accent is pure Cockney. 'It's a surprise, for our friend who's had chemo. She doesn't know a thing about it!'

There is light in her eyes.

'Come on!' says the Christmas tree. 'We've got to mark this in some way, this crazy day, this dance with death. It's only right!'

Kim finds herself laughing. She can't agree more.

This time next year, she will find the photo, four glammed-up friends in various poses outside the Crown Club. Daisy will remark how gorgeous they look, especially her mum. And for once, Kim will agree. There is dirt on her coat, but she looks radiant.

Looking at the photo, she will distil her exact feelings that night: how precious true friendship is, how rare. She will remember the moment of insight, the day's unlikely bequest – that the petty jealousies, the slights, real or imagined, that can stalk us all are such a waste of life.

Then they will turn to the other photo, the one pinned to the edge of the mirror. It's of Kim, a priest, a blind man and a woman in a headscarf. The priest is holding a present and the blind man tipping his glasses. Behind them, wrapping them in a huge papier-mâché hug, is a Christmas tree, between two baubles. At their feet is a sack of presents for a friend with cancer.

Daisy will ask why, after such an awful experience, their smiles are so wide.

Kim will think for a while. Something to do with relief, and memory, she'll say. That life is short and sometimes dark, but we shouldn't forget its gifts...

Daisy will nod and roll over. She will peer at the photo for a very long time, her head on one side.

'It made you remember,' she'll say.

Once Did Orla Davis...

Jesus is looking cranky. No one else sees this, cooing and smiling at him in admiration. But Tyler does, because he notices things. As the line of hopping children files past the stable scene, he brings his face up very close. Yep, cranky as hell. That's what his mum always says about his sister when she looks that way – forehead creased, mouth turned down, rigid arms with fist balls. Perhaps his nappy needs changing. Or he's hungry. Or he's in a bad mood for being born.

Mum says that about Elsie when she's cranky.

She's in a bad mood for being born. Tyler likes to hear the story because he comes out of it well. Elsie was late, so they inducted her (or was it infused?) but even then, she took ages to come out and in the end the doctor had to hoover her out with a vacuum thing. Whereas Tyler – Mum would ruffle his hair fondly at this point – came out bang on time. With little fuss and *no tearing.*

He doesn't really know what that means but it must be something to do with not ripping in two. Though when he told Orla Davis, she squeaked and shouted, 'It's to do with your mum, not you, numbskull! Ask her!' But he hasn't.

He likes the story the way it is. It cheers him up when he's feeling cross with Elsie, when it feels like she sucks up all the love in the house, leaving a space where his should be. When Mum tells the story, he feels special.

He stares at the Virgin Mary, pressing his face up close to the crib, wondering if Jesus had done it *without tearing.* Mary gazes back at him, calmly. She's not at all like his mum, he thinks, with her smooth skin, covered hair and patient expression. His mum has freckles and springy curls which she runs through her hands. She rushes around all day saying things like 'For Pete's sake!' and 'Hell's bells!' Unless she sits down – then she falls promptly asleep. She never used to be like this, before Elsie was born. But babies make you crazy, especially at six months old. This is what he's noticed. Particularly if you have a husband who works away. And a farty dog.

He stares glumly at Jesus, all small and cranky in his wooden crib, and then at his adoring parents. Joseph is on the edge of things behind a shepherd. Tyler reaches out grubby fingers and moves him closer to Jesus. He gives the baby a secret nod.

'At least your dad's here,' he tells him. 'Mine prob'ly won't be back till Christmas Eve. He'll miss the carols. Again.'

He sighs and pulls his head back away from the stable scene. But when he turns round, the line has gone. At the other end of the parish church, the rest of the class are jostling for places in the choir stalls. He makes to run and join them.

But Miss Flack is standing in front of him, hands on hips.

'*What* do you think you're doing, Tyler Ferguson?' Her face is red and her mouth working furiously. 'Did I actually see you *touch* him?'

'Sorry, Miss, touch who?'

Tyler glances around. He often gets in trouble for touching people, but there's no one around.

He squints up at the teacher. She's standing in a fall of light from the stained-glass window, her face a patchwork of coloured squares. He imagines pushing her over, face-first, into the paintbox he got for his birthday. He bats the thought away.

Miss Flack grows taller. She is thin with big hair, a furious isosceles triangle (they've just done shape in Maths and Tyler is pleased he can remember this). She looms over him, and he steps back into the crib scene. It wobbles dangerously.

'Stand still!' He freezes. 'I have told you,' she shouts, 'countless times not to *touch*!'

Tyler lifts his chin and tries to look at her. He is scared of her – they all are – and he can't quite bring himself to meet her eye. He says nothing. There is no point. Mis Flack hates him. This is because he never gets things right. Somehow, he gets the wrong end of the stick, misunderstands, doesn't listen.

Miss Flack teaches them when their teacher is away which, horrifyingly, is all the time now as Mrs James is in Critical Care. At least, that's what it said in the school newsletter. Tyler knows the word 'criticise' (from the Year 5/6 spelling list) but can't work out why it's being used for lovely Mrs James. She went in for a heart op. Also, she's so kind, he can't imagine her criticising anyone, especially those caring for her. But there you are. It is one of life's mysteries.

Miss Flack is one of those teachers who talk a lot; she likes her own voice but no one else's. If anyone puts up a hand to ask questions, she frowns and waves it down as if swatting a fly. She doesn't like anything getting in the way of her explanations, which are long and very boring. In fact, she doesn't seem to like children at all (apart from Orla). Tyler is sure if she stood talking at the front, by the interactive whiteboard (which she hates and never uses) in an empty classroom, she'd be happy.

What's weird is that whenever Mrs Bright, their head teacher, comes into class, she changes completely, smiling at everyone and asking questions. *Can anyone explain that back to me? Who would like to show me on the board?* Her face goes all warm and crinkly and she turns a bit red. And Mrs Bright (who's not very) always seems *persuaded* (another spelling word) and tiptoes out again.

Once, Tyler nearly shouted 'Don't go, she's a witch!' It was so hard not to that he had to cough into his hand to stop himself. He knows it would do no good. Mrs Bright is always saying that schools like theirs are lucky to have a great teacher like Miss Flack. Long-term supplies are hard to find. Tyler doesn't understand this. Supplies are delivered in a big lorry that beeps for ages when reversing into the car park.

Suddenly, Orla is there, skipping and hopping, calling up to Miss Flack in her sing-song voice.

'Miss, Miss, we have to get in our groups. Mr Lamb said!'

Miss Flack looks down at Orla and her face softens. Tyler thinks for the thousandth time how lucky Orla is. Everyone adores her – the teachers, the parents, other children. There's something about her blue eyes, her easy smile, that draws people. They want to be near her. She can even win over Miss Flack, who Tyler knows she hates.

'Thanks, sweetheart,' says the teacher. She glares at Tyler. 'Off you go, then!' Tyler scarpers.

Orla loops her arm through his as they walk as fast as they can towards the little group standing in the middle of the aisle.

'Silly cow,' she mutters, her face close to his ear. 'If God didn't want us to touch, why did he give us hands?'

Tyler shrugs. It's another mystery, along with why Orla is his friend and chillies aren't called hotties.

'Ah, there you are, Tyler!' Mr Lamb is sorting out who stands where. He has a beard and kind eyes, so even when he's telling them off, no one minds. But this could be partly because they're fascinated by the way his mouth moves when he's upset, dislodging bits of toast or dried egg from recent meals. Now, he's gently pushing each child into position with the tip of his finger while consulting sheets on a clipboard. Tyler peers at the beard hopefully. No food in sight.

He looks up at the church ceiling while he waits his turn. There are big, curving ridges way up high. They fan out with huge, webbed feet like the ducks they feed on the way home from school. He tips his head back, hypnotised by the patterns and swirls which leap and twist above him. Suddenly he's falling.

As he tips to one side, everything begins to swim. Orla grabs him.

'What are you doing, idiot?' Orla is always calling him names in her warm, laughing voice. He never understood why until he went to play at her house. Her mum, who, unlike his, spends most of her time lying on the sofa with magazines, did the same. His own mum had said that when you have six children, perhaps it was the only way.

He rights himself and the dizziness goes.

'Have you ever looked at a high ceiling for a long time?' he asks her. 'You fall up.'

Orla rolls her eyes. 'You don't fall up, numbskull,' she says. 'You just get dizzy.'

At that point, the vicar arrives and the last few are hurried into position by Mr Lamb: Tyler on the back row – 'because you're tall,' Mr Lamb says – and Orla at the front; she's doing the solo. The vicar settles himself in the front pew next to Miss Flack. Having greeted him with her Mrs-Bright-face, she is now staring fiercely at the children. Tyler catches her eye and jerks his body into a more upright position, as if electrified. This generally goes down well with teachers. But Miss Flack carries on glaring.

She had warned them several times that the vicar would be coming to the dress rehearsal and would be *wanting perfection*. Tyler's heart sinks. He finds it so hard to stand still, to concentrate, to do all the things the others seem to be able to do. Perhaps there's something wrong with him.

Then he remembers that the vicar, who they know from Sundays, is Mum's friend. He's funny and kind and wears a leather jacket, sometimes even when he's preaching. *Lovely Aidan.* That's what Mum calls him. Surely he will understand.

Mr Lamb taps his stick on the music stand. The sound it makes is clear as a bell. The children fall silent, even the ones in the choir stalls behind them.

Miss Flack, the vicar and a lady arranging flowers all look at the little group at the front. Orla draws a breath. Mr Lamb plays a note on the recorder.

Orla opens her mouth and starts to sing.

Tyler keeps meaning to ask why she's singing those words. But no one seems to mind. In fact, they love it. The lady with flowers puts them down and sinks into a pew to listen. The vicar stares dreamily at the ceiling. As for Miss Flack – and he peers at her to check this – her eyes look like Mum's after phone calls with Dad: shiny.

Beneath Orla's voice, there's a loud hush. It rolls towards him like a wave. The singing, clearer and fuller than in the classroom, makes him want to look up, to have that strange, falling feeling again. He tries to resist. But Orla's voice rises, Miss Flack wipes her eyes, and the wave rolls over him.

He can't stop himself. His eyes are pulled up towards the soaring space, the web of ridges, the emptiness. And, as Orla's voice reaches the high note, he tips his head back. And falls.

If he'd realised how much it would hurt, perhaps he wouldn't have done it. But, lying there on the floor, next to the stone thing they use to wet babies, now stained with blood from where his head hit, he's not so sure. He always does stupid things. He can't seem to help it.

The teachers spring into action, getting the children out of the area. Lovely Aidan sits with Tyler and holds his hand. He says kind things like 'Everything will be fine' and 'Try not to worry'. He is holding something a bit too tight on Tyler's head.

'Am I going to bleed to death?' Tyler wonders. He's seen this happen on *Casualty*.

'Absolutely not!' says Aidan, changing hands and moving his position so he can ease Tyler's head gently into his lap. 'The ambulance will be here before you can say Jack Robinson...'

Tyler has no idea who Jack is. He can see the vicar's other hand is red with blood. It reminds him of the picture he showed them at school in an RE lesson about Easter. Jesus on a cross and a lot of blood. He couldn't look then, and he can't now.

Above him, the spaces between the ridges are getting smaller. It strikes him as interesting that he wanted to look up. Now it's all he can do.

The ridges swim closer and closer together, shape-shifting into isosceles triangles. Briefly, he sees Miss Flack looking down at him, her face grim.

And then, nothing.

When he opens his eyes, he's on a stretcher and above him is an upside-down person in green. She has a ponytail and blue eyes.

'Hello, Tyler,' she smiles. 'You gave everyone a shock back there!'

His head is on one side, the good side. He tries to work out where he is. Open-mouthed children, held back by Mr Lamb, are watching his journey down the aisle. A deep ache is throbbing in his head. The stretcher is carried past the crib with cranky Jesus. *Don't let me die*, he tells him.

He can hear Orla shouting in the distance and Miss Flack trying to calm her.

'Let me go!' Orla's voice is angry but faint. 'Let. Me. Go. With him!' Then he slides away again on a sea of nothing, where birds soar across the ceiling above and the ridges shift, Harry-Potter-like, into more isosceles triangles, which reform into a hundred Miss Flacks.

When he next opens his eyes, he's in a white room and one of the Miss Flacks is peering over him. It can't be the usual one because this Miss Flack is looking worried, not angry.

'Which one are you?' he asks.

She frowns and speaks to someone close by. 'I think he's delirious,' she says.

Another face appears, a man with glasses and too-big eyes. The person speaks but the voice is too far away; he can't hear what he's saying.

The people in the white room come and go; there are strange noises – buzzes and beeps and in the distance, once, a siren – and a funny smell.

Tyler dreams of opening his front door to find Dad there: ridiculously tall Dad with his big smile and dark eyes, scooping him up and swinging him round and hugging him until he can't breathe. Then they go inside, and Dad opens a case full of Christmas presents for him and Elsie. But he doesn't care about them. He just wants to hang with Dad, to roll on the floor, to play-fight, to show him the spelling list where he got ten out of ten and a *Well done, Tyler!* with a sticker at the bottom. He wants to tell Dad that two people are better than one when there's a baby involved, because babies make you crazy. In his dream, he can feel their home filling up the way it's meant to, a balloon finally taking shape.

*

But when he opens his eyes, he's in the white room again and there's a funny feeling by his ear.

He tries to sit up but is gently pushed down again. The man with the glasses is speaking. Tyler frowns. Standing behind the man, looking at Tyler with concerned eyes, is Miss Flack.

The man is fiddling with something next to his ear while his head feels hot and strange. He lifts a hand and touches something thick where the blood came from.

'I didn't die,' he tells the man.

'Nope.' He fiddles again with the thing behind his ear and stands up. 'I'm Doctor Simms, Tyler. Good to see you awake.'

Tyler winces. Everything's so loud: the doctor, the beeps and buzzes, the person groaning in the bed next to him.

He puts a hand over one ear. The doctor glances at Miss Flack and sits down next to him.

'Is my mum coming?' he asks them.

Miss Flack leans over the doctor's shoulder. 'We're trying to get hold of her, Tyler. A neighbour said she works in the café on Fridays. But no one knows which one. Do you?'

Tyler thinks. On Fridays, Mum drops him at school and then takes Elsie to the childminder. Their café is on the corner by the main road. Orla's mum drops him off after school. It has a big window and a white sign with green sloping writing. At each corner of the sign there is a small tree. What's the name between them? He tries to see it in his mind, but his head is thick and fuzzy like he's headed a football.

'The Olive Tree!' It comes to him quickly. Yes, that's it. He winces again at the sound of his voice but is pleased he's remembered. His head aches with the effort and he feels hot. He thinks of the big walk-in fridge at the Olive Tree where he was once sent to get milk. He imagines moving all the milk off the lowest shelf, which is as deep as the bunk in his room at home. He'd like to lie down on that shelf and let the cold cover him.

'Tyler!' He looks up. Miss Flack has gone, and the doctor is looking at him with those too-big eyes. He pushes his glasses further up his nose. He has hairy fingers. 'Can you remember what happened?'

Tyler puts a hand to his head and feels the bandage. 'I fell,' he says. 'In the church when we were rehearsing for the vicar.'

The doctor nods and smiles. 'You did,' he agrees, 'and you hit your head on the font. The big stone thing behind you,' he adds just to be clear. 'How are you feeling?'

Tyler thinks of the strange, soaring feeling of falling up when he'd tipped his head. Should he tell the doctor about that? But he hears Orla's urgent voice in his ear, as he does every day in class, *Just answer the question, Tyler.*

'I've got a headache,' he tells the doctor.

Doctor Simms nods. 'That will go,' he says. 'Don't worry. And the reason everything's loud,' he adds, 'is because I looked in your ear; there was lot of blood there. It turns out you've had multiple ear infections, and it's affected your hearing. I've given you a trial hearing aid.'

After Mum has arrived and hugged and cried over him, and Miss Flack has been thanked and the doctor questioned so much that his glasses steam up (and his eyes completely disappear), they're allowed to go. Mum holds Tyler's hand and carries a bag of medicine and a long list of instructions. His head feels about three times bigger than it's meant to be, and the world, usually distant and unreachable, is now right there, shouting for attention.

As they walk slowly towards the car, they pass a whistling man, a barking dog, a child shouting 'Batman!' His feet thud; leaves whisper on trees. He gazes up at them in awe. He tips his head back to look and feels a bit dizzy. He grips Mum's hand, and she tells him to keep his head straight because of the wound.

What an adventure he's had today. He can't wait to get back to school to tell them. Mum says if he's good and rests properly, he might even be there in time for the carol service.

On the big day, Orla, who's hardly left his side since he got back, tells him Miss Flack will be there. Her mother knows someone who knows her. She left after Tyler's fall, upset to think she hadn't spotted his deafness and got cross instead. Tyler was glad, until Orla added that apparently Miss Flack was not well herself. 'Not well in the head,' Orla had whispered. Miss Flack's dad, who she'd cared for, had just died of cancer. She probably shouldn't have been teaching at all. Tyler thinks of the teacher's angry face, of her leaky eyes while Orla sang. So strange that teachers have homes and dads and can be sad or scared like children. That teachers have feelings too.

The church is full when Mrs Bright stands up in her grey suit and welcomes everyone to the school's annual carol service. Tyler notices she's wearing a blouse covered in Christmas trees. When it's Year 6's turn, he gets up from the second pew and walks in a line to the front where his group stand. He walks tall and doesn't wobble once.

When he reaches his place, he stares out at the many people in front of them: teachers, parents, grandparents, eagerly waiting to see their child perform. He scans the crowd but can't see Mum. Everyone else's family will be there. He can see Orla's mum and dad and her big brother and sisters and Miss Flack, her head bent over the carol sheet. But no one for him. He sighs. Elsie must have stopped her coming. Again.

Mr Lamb taps his stick on the music stand and there is a hush so deep he could climb into it. He watches the back of Orla's head. It rises a bit as she takes a breath. She begins to sing. And as soon as the first notes, clear and cool, glide through the air above them, he realises. Because he can hear every word.

It's not 'Once did Orla Davis sit here…' and never has been.

'Once in Royal David's City,' sings Orla, 'stood a lowly cattle shed…'

The hush rolls towards him again. His eyes are drawn up, up to the huge ceiling with its webbed arches, the sound pulling him away from the people down here. He tips his head back but this time he's not dizzy. He doesn't fall.

He lowers his head and tries to focus, to get ready for the fourth verse with the rest of the group. But he can't stop thinking about that first line. How could he have got it wrong for so long?

Once did Orla Davis sit here… If it hadn't been for Orla sitting next to him all this time, he would never have coped. He'd got so much wrong because he hadn't heard, but Orla had covered for him and helped him. Perhaps he'd thought it was worth singing about.

It's only when he hears his own voice, in the fourth verse, that he sees them. They're sitting on the side near the front.

Tyler is filled with pride. He grows a little taller, opens his mouth wider.

'…he was little, weak and helpless, tears and smiles like us he knew…'

He sings for cranky Jesus and sad Miss Flack; for kind Orla and Lovely Aidan; for Mum with her phone-tears and hospital-hugs.

But mostly he sings for the person next to her, the tall one with the dark eyes and big smile.

'…And he feeleth for our sadness, and he shareth in our gladness.'

And his voice has never been so big and beautiful.

The Chain

It's reached the point where there's chaos everywhere. Rooms strewn with stuff, half-filled boxes, gap-toothed walls where pictures once were. Mum is sitting on the sofa, head in her hands. Which takes some doing when you're wedged between a mirror and a Meccano model of the Eiffel Tower (which we promised we'd leave intact. Bad idea).

It's been worse for Noah, though. That's what I tell myself when I resent the allowances we make for him, *the longed-for second child*. I've called him this for years, but I'll have to stop now. To lose your dad and your home (twice) is hard at any age, but when you're ten, it robs you of your unshakeable confidence in life's goodness. Kids need that.

On top of everything else, it's three days to Christmas, the best time for a child to move house. Said no one, ever.

I stare through the curtainless windows. Outside, the afternoon shifts and yawns. It's very cold, but the heating doesn't come on until four and we're trying to save money. A few lazy flakes of snow zigzag down, slow at first, then fast, the way ideas are born.

The neighbour's teenagers slouch past the window, their rucksacks dragging. Those school days seem endless, but what I wouldn't give to have them back again – the freedom, the lack of responsibility. If Dad were alive, would it still be that way? Probably. I feel a surge of rage at him for dying. We could *really* have done without it.

I get a grip – someone has to – and touch Mum's shoulder. 'Tea?'

She sighs and lifts her head. Her long hair is tied back off her face. It makes her look fragile.

'Thanks, love.' She looks exhausted. 'I think we're at the stage where we ignore which boxes are for which room in the new house and just stuff it all in anywhere.'

'But tea first,' I say, heading for the kitchen. I marvel how good I am at adulting. That's what uni does for you if you're anxious and don't like drinking games.

When the doorbell goes, it's dark but we've nearly finished. The throw-it-in-anyhow method has worked. The flat is empty of our individual personalities and full of identical boxes. It wears the blank expression of a friend you've stopped talking to. This is the second move in a year (third for me, if you count uni) but it still surprises me how unsettling it is.

Mum collapses on the sofa again, breaking off a corner of the Eiffel Tower. It lurches wonkily to one side.

'*Attention*!' I call in my best French accent and make for the door. It's not a huge flat so you can hear pretty much everything from everywhere.

'Ah!' says the solicitor, almost before I've got the door open. Mum says he's technically an articled clerk – training to be a solicitor.

There's a rush of dread and cold air. I'm not an expert in house-moving glitches but even I know solicitors don't usually visit the day before completion. He's wearing a suit and a grave expression, even though it's 9pm.

'Ruby, isn't it? Can I come in?'

He's nice enough, Mum's solicitor; this is his son, who's alright too. He's one of those guys whose face is too young for the rest of him, as though he's dressed in his dad's clothes. Perhaps he is.

He's employed by him after all and is doing much of the work for the sale.

He shifts from foot to foot and coughs, covering his face briefly. His eyes look uncertain. 'There's something I need to discuss with your mum,' he says.

'Is... is it bad?' I stutter, thinking of the boxes and how shattered she is.

The guy looks at me. I remember his name is Steve.

'It's not great, Ruby,' he says, his voice all low and serious. 'It's an issue with the chain. But it can be sorted.'

I'm impressed he's remembered my name; we've only met once. I open the door wider and gesture for him to come through to the lounge. But Mum is already on her feet beside me. I close the door and we stand there in the hall, while he tells us. His voice is filled with professional regret. This does not make it easier.

When he's finished, and Mum has burst into tears of fatigue and despair, we go through to the lounge. I put the kettle on while Mum wipes her eyes and tries to get a grip. I've seen this before but once she's started, she can't stop. She's very emotional for a counsellor. It intrigues me that she's so in demand. Perhaps because she feels so deeply, she relates to others well.

When I return with a tray of mugs, she's back by the Eiffel Tower while Steve is standing near the door looking awkward. Planning his escape?

I put the tray on top of a box and clear an armchair of Aldi bags filled with plants.

'Could it get sorted by tomorrow?' she asks, her nostrils bubbling. She's had a cold for as long as I can remember. It started when Dad died, two years ago.

'Probably not tomorrow, Esther,' says Steve. He perches on the edge of the chair, accepts a mug of tea while managing to look both sympathetic and reluctant.

'Not until after Christmas now... But hopefully in the New Year,' he adds, as Mum starts to sob again.

Thank goodness Noah's at his friend's. He'd be beside himself.

'It's not that unusual,' says Steve the Solicitor. Calling him that makes me think of Allan Ahlberg. How Noah and I both loved that *Happy Families* series. Shame we aren't one any more.

'The chain can break down at any point,' he continues, 'and while it rarely happens this late in the day, there's always a risk.'

'So what the hell are we supposed to do?' says Mum, her voice rising with each syllable. Her eyes are leaking all over her white jumper. 'We have to leave the flat but can't move into the house. And tomorrow the removals arrive. Christmas in the van, is it?'

She jerks her arm around to indicate our three lives spread around the room like some crazy 3D jigsaw. It would make a good quiz. Question: What's that pink thing poking out of the box? Answer: Mum's going-out bra, not to be confused with her going-up bra which makes everything 'a bit more perky'.

The solicitor puts down his tea and wipes his face with a massive handkerchief. He looks awkward. *My most hysterical customer.* He could write a piece for the *Solicitors' Gazette* if there is one. But who can blame her? We've got to return the keys of our rented flat by tomorrow afternoon and the removal van will be here first thing in the morning.

Steve picks up his mug and sits further back on the chair for emotional protection. Behind him, propped against the wall, is a framed piece of calligraphy (Mum's hobby when she's not fixing people). 'There's no place like home,' it reads. Quite.

'It's inconvenient,' he says, 'I'm aware of that. But I assure you I've done all I can. At least you found out today and not tomorrow...'

I thought the guys at uni lacked emotional intelligence cos they're young and stupid. There are clearly older stupid guys too. Mum, impressively, ignores this.

'Why didn't you alert us earlier?' she demands.

'It only came to light today,' he says. 'I spent all afternoon working on it but I assure you, Esther, there's nothing we can do. It's an admin error further up the chain, which means the mortgage approval for your vendor's vendor has been delayed and their funds can't be released.'

He sighs. 'Is there anywhere you can stay for a bit?' He looks at us both hopefully. 'Someone with an empty double garage or something?'

Mum glares. 'Yeah, I've got loads of friends like that,' she says. 'No one stores stuff in the garage these days.'

The solicitor sighs. 'There must be someone. You're lucky we were alerted before removals arrive,' he adds.

At this point Mum looks thunderous and I decide to calm things down a bit. 'What about Judith?' I offer.

'What?' She's still glaring at the solicitor who is, finally, looking embarrassed.

'Judith,' I say again. 'She's the obvious person to ask. To stay with. Until it's fixed, I mean.'

Mum blows out a breath and it goes on so long I worry she's forgotten the part about reoxygenation. She puts her hands over her face, making the Eiffel Tower rock alarmingly. Hunched on the edge of the sofa, in green leggings and a red cardi, she looks like a demented elf.

I take charge. 'I'm ringing Judith,' I tell her, and turn to the solicitor. 'Thank you for your help. We'll be in touch.' It doesn't sound quite right but it's the kind of thing Mum says to people on the phone and, let's face it, I'm only eighteen and learning how to do life. *Go away* is what I really mean. *You're upsetting Mum.*

Steve looks both relieved and confused. I've stolen his words and now he's out of sync.

'Er... no, *we'll* be in touch,' he says, 'once things have been sorted.' He puts his mug on the tray, stands up, hovers uncertainly. I put my own mug down and walk briskly to the door, which is hard when the room's not that big and you're navigating boxes. But I want to make it clear the visit is over.

In the hall, I open the door and stand well back. He nods at me as he leaves.

'Happy Christmas,' he mumbles vaguely.

'Well, it won't be,' I call after him as he walks towards his BMW, which will no doubt take him back to his nice house and nice family this December evening. If he has children, I hope they're glad he's not dead. I glare at him until he's driven off. Then I go back inside, move what's left of the model and sit down next to Mum. I put an arm round her.

It's always like this, even though I'm the one with anxiety. That's because it's social anxiety (going to lectures, cooking in communal kitchens, talking to other students) so with this sort of thing (being homeless) I seem to cope. *You're a lion on the inside, Ruby.* That's what the counsellor said when I told her about kicking Max at school for bullying a Polish kid. *Let the lion out!*

I told her it's hard to be more lion when your outer mouse is in charge.

At least it's warm in the flat now. And we've pretty much finished packing. I sit next to Mum and listen to the voice inside that tells me what to do. Outside, a dog barks; from the kitchen, there's the hum of the fridge – the obscure comfort of ordinary things.

Of this I am sure: the chain, with all its power to depress and defeat, will not win. Because although there are fewer of us, we're still a family. As soon as I think this, I am sure it's the right thing to do.

'Look, Mum,' I say, 'Judith will be fine about this, and she has that big old barn thing where they could put the stuff. It might only be for two weeks or so. Shall I ring her?'

You would think she'd have suggested this herself. But our relationship with Dad's mum has always been... difficult. It's not the time to dwell on that, though.

Mum wipes her eyes with the sleeve of her cardi, which is difficult because it's too thick and a bit hairy. I rummage in my pocket for a tissue but can't find one. We both remember at the same moment that it was Dad who always produced tissues when needed. One of those little packs would announce itself with a flourish, apparently from nowhere, like a magic trick.

Suddenly and inappropriately, we both crack up. If Steve was still here, he'd stare. The thought of this makes me laugh harder.

'Do you remember,' wheezes Mum, 'how he used to have that stupid look of pride every time he did it?'

'Like he'd just won the lottery.'

We both start to rock, tears pouring down our faces. It's a release after the stress of the day, and the realisation that everything will probably be OK. We've been through it a bit recently, our family.

We get a grip and calm down. Mum will be alright now. She's funny that way.

Ashdown House is in the middle of a forest. It's big and gloomy, but was grand in the old days. Now it looks like something from a low-budget horror movie. It's almost dark because the removal men had to speak to their boss and he was in a meeting, so having waited and rung twice more, his PA, who is also his wife, had to make the decision. Anyway, it got sorted in the end and we follow the lights of the lorry as it lumbers out of town, up the hill, through the woods to the narrow lane, and into the drive of the big house.

So many memories from coming here as kids. We adored the place. The grounds are huge, there's a lake you can swim in and a tower which I took Noah up when I was twelve and he was four. We made our own bows and arrows, and I showed him how archers used to defend the place. There was a hairy moment when he leaned over the battlements to see where the arrow went. Good that I grabbed him but not good that he told Mum at bedtime that he 'nearly flew today'. From then on, the top door of the tower was locked for years.

Noah still loves it here. But I find it depressing. From the moment we turned into the drive, Dad would spend the whole time pointing things out – the trees he'd climbed, where he'd found rabbits, and where he'd swum in the lake at Christmas. Those stories come back to me now as we pass each place, reminding me he's not here to tell them. Dad – easy-going, jokey – *how can you not be in the world any more?* It makes no actual sense.

'How long can we stay?' asks Noah. He's twisting his comfort-dog in his hands. It's old and smelly and, at ten, he really shouldn't have it. But like us, he's still trying to find a way through. To navigate the insanity of losing Dad.

As Mum drives carefully around the roundabout thing at the top (who has a roundabout in their drive?), she tells him, in her too-bright voice, that it depends.

'Hopefully, two weeks or so,' she lies. I know she hopes it's less.

Judith, Dad's mum (we're not allowed to call her Granny), is a bit scary, but only because she's posh and old and speaks her mind when she shouldn't. She's a bit of a legend, though, one of the brains behind the Reclaim the Night movement in the 1970s when women marched for their right to be safe. Now, in her eighties, she doesn't campaign much but still supports those who do.

One summer, we woke up to find people lying all over the Green Room floor. They were on their way to a pro-refugee demo in Brighton. At breakfast, one of them gave me a T-shirt which had 'Sorry about our prime minister' printed on it in big, black letters. Mum took it away. When I cried and asked her why, she said it wasn't the kind of thing you wore if your parents were in private practice.

Mum has never really got on with Judith, but things are a bit better these days. Mainly because when Dad died (cancer – sudden – unbearable), and we had to move to the flat, Judith managed to unlock some money from Grandad's estate (lawyer – investments – also dead). She gave it to us back in the summer so we could buy a house, which Mum eventually found in the autumn. I was at uni by then, trying not to cry myself to sleep or talk to people.

Mum parks near the van and we get out. Noah runs to the double doors and lifts the knocker. It's big and heavy with the face of a lion. No one likes it because of its angry stare. When knocked, it makes a massive noise only he can get away with.

It's dark now. Light falls through coloured glass, throwing pink and green shapes at our faces. The lamps by the porch and either side of the roundabout are bright with welcome. There's nothing quite like the dark out here in the forest, and even a little light makes a big difference. As we wait for Judith or Al to open up, I tip my head back and stare at the sky. The stars are super-bright and scattered, glitter tipped on velvet.

The removal men have already opened the back doors of the lorry and started taking things out. I can see the outline of my desk and Noah's Lego table. They look a bit lost, and much smaller than usual.

At last Judith opens the door.

'Darlings, you must be exhausted. Great to have you.' She's wearing a red and green kilt and a tight smile, the sort that makes you think she means the opposite – but she probably doesn't. We go in, Noah racing ahead to see what's changed since we were last here, Mum dragging one case, me the other. Judith goes out and starts telling the removal men where to put our stuff – in the old stable block which has lain empty for a while, but is thankfully watertight, we hear her say.

We pull our cases into the hall, leaving the men's objections outside in the cold air. They soon falter when Judith tells them in her strident voice that she knows their boss and they'll be out of a job if they don't shift it. This may or may not be true.

When she's finished, Judith comes back in and hugs Mum and me. She walks more slowly than she used to. Noah is nowhere to be seen.

'I put Noah in the little room,' she says (it's not little at all). 'Esther, you're in your usual, but I've had to move you, Ruby. The damp up there is getting worse and it's not good for you.'

I shrug. I'm not as crazy about the tower as I used to be. Dad used to hide in the cupboard by the stairs and jump out at me. When I was older, he'd stand at the window pointing out bits of the forest and telling me their names – Dreamers' Vale, the Magic Mound, Puddlesford. Now he's gone, it's like the places have gone too, sucked of the stories that brought them to life.

When we've dumped the cases in our rooms – mine's the Red Room, full of dark furniture and rugs – we find Noah and go downstairs for dinner. The grand staircase, I notice, with its sweeping banisters and huge window, has a hole in the carpet. The suit of armour at the bottom, in which Dad once hid from guests, needs a polish. I give it a pat.

We eat in the dining room. It's crazy cold, despite the fire, and the table is too big for four. Judith has put out what she calls the 'best candelabra' and must have done the food herself, Al being on leave. It's unbelievable, Mum always says, that there are people living like Downton Abbey in this day and age. But that's not really fair. Judith might be a bit grand, but the house is freezing, the roof leaks and although she doesn't cook, she eats in the kitchen with Al.

But Mum was brought up on a council estate and worked like a dog to get where she is. She resents everything Judith stands for.

'Well, that's that, then!' says Judith, after the meal, clapping her hands cos she's forgotten Al's away. Mum drags herself to her feet, but I push her down.

'Mum, you and Noah go to bed. You must be knackered.' I can see Judith raise her eyebrows. 'I'll sort this.'

I start collecting the dirty plates and empty dishes. Mum nods and taps Noah on the shoulder. We hear him complaining all the way up the grand staircase.

Judith and I put everything onto the trolley, and I wheel it through the other door and along the Turkish carpet to the kitchen. It's an ancient room, small compared to the dining room, but with a high ceiling and retro fittings. Except they're 1950s and the real thing.

I pile it all into the massive sink with a generous squirt of Fairy, and turn on the taps.

'Why don't you get a dishwasher?' I ask Judith.

She snorts. 'I don't need one,' she replies, all curt and Judith-like. 'I've got Al.'

I want to remind her that Al isn't here. And to ask why, as someone who supports every minority group on the planet, she can't extend a bit of thought for her ageing servant. Because, although they're more like friends these days, that's basically what he is.

We wash and wipe in silence. The kitchen smells worryingly of gas. The fridge, an ancient-looking contraption in the corner, hums erratically, but Judith is proud of its low carbon footprint. Shame it doesn't keep things cold. Mind you, the kitchen does that on its own.

I step back to wipe my hands and my feet squeak on the sticky floor. I glance at the worktops and see lumps of pasta sauce. I think briefly of Marcos, with whom I bonded over the disgusting kitchen at uni. With OCD, he found it harder to go in there than I did. When I found him cowering by the door in tears, I barged in and told everyone we needed a cleaning rota. They stared at me, open-mouthed, shrugged, nodded. So I made one and monitor it ruthlessly.

I run the water, rinse the cloth and wipe down the side. Judith leans against the dresser and watches me.

'You must be tired, Ruby.'

I shrug. I should be after the drama of the day, but the last thing I feel like doing is sleeping. And it's only 10pm. That's nothing in uni-time, even for people with social anxiety. While the others party in the kitchen, I'm reading or studying in my room. There's no point trying to sleep.

'Thanks for the food,' I tell her. I won't meet her eye in case I see pity, but it's unlikely. Judith is a coper and expects others to be. When we were little, if we fell over or fell out, she was coldly dismissive.

'Get up and get over it,' she'd say. 'There are worse things in life.' We never asked what they are. I guess we know now.

'Sleep well, Ruby,' she says. And as I turn for the door, quietly, she says something else. I turn back and for a moment catch a glimpse of another Judith, a milder one, whose features are less sharp, blurred with some emotion. But before I can decide what it is, the expression has gone, the mask in place.

'See you in the morning,' she says. 'I'm off to bed, too.'

I walk through the kitchen door, pretending not to hear her, and feel a surge of annoyance. My grandmother, so strong and unyielding, has always been both scary and reassuring, mainly because you know what to expect from her. But now, just for once, it would be great if she'd open her arms so I could run into them, lean on her, feel her strength, be carried by it. Even cry with her. For a heartbeat, I thought it might happen.

I trudge up the grand staircase, wondering whether loss has created such determined optimism. Dad once said his mother had so much strength, it spilled over into other people. No setback ever throws her off course. Like when she 'had to let the gardener go': she was determined she could do his job herself, and she has, only taking on others for the heavy work.

I walk past the Red Room, up the back stairs and along the short corridor to the door of the tower. It's very still. Only the muted scream of water coursing through the pipes in some part of the house. Probably Judith in her ancient bathroom.

There's no key in the door, but the tower isn't locked these days. It's strange climbing the twisty stairs to Dad's old room, but I put my hand on the cold stone wall and feel supported, reassured. The house was built in the eighteenth century. It's a bit old, a bit run-down, but it's still here.

I open the door at the top and switch on the light. The Round Room is as shabby as ever, with its heavy drapes and wooden furniture. I've always loved the curved chest of drawers with its mottled mirror, specially made to fit the room. The walls hold framed drawings of Dad's and a photo of me and Noah splashing in the lake. It was so long ago I can hardly remember.

But it's the view that makes this room special. There are four windows which give the most amazing outlook across the forest, towards London on one side, the downs on the other. I walk to the nearest window and lean my head on the glass, staring into the night. I think of the forest unrolling into the darkness, the birds and animals it shelters, the dwellings. The tops of the trees are a mass of dark shapes knitted together across chinks of light. If you zoomed up and out, you'd see southern England, bigger swathes of darkness, and London, a smear of gold with smaller smudges flickering above it. And then, up, up, looking down on our world – a ball flung in space. How does it stay up there?

I do this sometimes. At uni, it makes me afraid, the vastness and the smallness. But here, in the forest, I've always felt safe. More so now I'm bereaved, homeless, anxious and hating student life. I sigh and turn towards the bed. Its sagging familiarity is somehow soothing, and I throw myself onto it. There's something hard sticking up below the mattress. I roll over and land on all fours, peering into the dust underneath. There's a box. Bending low, half cricking my neck, I pull it out.

We sit together in the middle of the floor, the box and I, and look at each other. It's not big but it's heavy and tied with string. It has a shouty label on the top which says *PRIVATE*. I observe it from different angles, wondering what the label means. Private as far as anyone in the house is concerned? Or private as far as non-family is concerned? I decide on the latter. Maybe it contains interesting arte-facts from Dad's past, though the writing is definitely not his. For a start, you can read it.

I lift the box onto the bed and sit next to it. The string pulls apart easily. I am lifting the flaps, bending them back so they don't close again, when the door creaks. And Judith walks in.

I flinch and feel hot all over. For some reason it never occurred to me she wasn't tucked up in her ridiculous bed with the huge curtains and heavy quilts. Duvets never made it to Ashdown House.

She stands there in the doorway, in her dressing gown. Her grey hair is loose across her shoulders, her eyes like glitter. *Great, I've done it now.*

'I thought you were in bed,' I tell her.

'Clearly.' She doesn't make things easy for you, Judith.

We stay like that for a bit, me on the bed, holding a flap of the box, she in her red dressing gown with a face of stone, trying to hide the fact she's panting a little from the climb.

'Look, I'm sorry,' I say. 'I just lay on the bed, and it was sticking up. I shouldn't have opened it but, you know, I was curious. Human nature, isn't it?'

There's a beat in which I can't decide which way it will go. Her face changes.

'It's alright, Ruby. I was going to show you anyway, and I would have done tonight if you hadn't had such a rough day.'

She closes the door and comes to sit opposite me on the bed, folding her legs beneath her the way younger people do. She looks at the box and I wonder what to do next. All I can see is a few dusty containers and on top, a smaller box of faded velvet, a jewellery box.

'Is this Dad's stuff?'

She looks at me then. 'No, Ruby, it's mine. There's enough at Ashdown House to remind you of your father. I'd hardly make things worse.'

As she looks down, I can see the shadows on her face, the sunken eyes. Strands of hair twist around her neck and there's a spit of saliva on her lip. In her nightwear she looks – this is unheard of – vulnerable. The doggedness is gone; sadness cups her face. The fearless campaigner, the lady of the manor, the dis-approving grandmother, they've left. There's just an old woman who's lost a husband and a son.

A lump the size of a golf ball fattens my throat. I gulp it down. I wanted to see the real Judith. I'm not so sure now.

'What's in it?' I ask her. My voice wobbles.

She reaches down and picks up the velvet box. 'Memories,' she says. 'But this one – this one, Ruby, is a bit special. And it's for you.'

Her hands are like crumpled paper, cool to the touch. I put the box on my knee, touch its worn velvet. I lift the lid. Inside is a pendant on a silver chain. It's old but has been highly polished and winks in the light from the bulb above. I bring it closer to my face so I can examine it.

'It's the door knocker!'

Judith nods. 'That's right. Can you see the writing around the edge?'

I peer at it, turning the pendant this way and that in the dim light. It's something in Latin. 'What does it mean?'

The pendant on its silver chain is beautiful, the lion's face kinder and its mane smoother than the one on the door. All you want to do is stroke the shiny face with a finger. And the chain is slender but strong, made of twisted loops that gleam in the dull light.

Judith closes the bigger box and pushes it to the side. She sits back against the headboard.

'It means "Trust who you're meant to be",' she says. 'It's written on the knocker too, but it's so rubbed away now you can hardly see.'

She watches me as I unfasten the little clip and put the beautiful chain around my neck. It falls just shy of my cleavage. There's something comforting about the weight of it against my chest. Steadying.

'It's beautiful,' I tell her. 'Why haven't I seen it before?'

Judith shifts and settles herself. She rubs her back.

'I was given it, then I gave it to your father. Now it's yours.'

She turns her head to look out of the window.

'My grandfather had the pendant part made for my father as a tie pin,' she says. 'It was intended to remind him of his destiny as head of a large estate. In those days, you had responsibility: to the family, the whole area. You had a role. Then when I came of age, my father had it converted to a pendant and chain and gave it to me.'

'Did you wear it?' I ask her.

Judith turns her head. There's a faraway look in her eyes. She glances down at her hands, bony and old but glittering with the rings she wears. She stretches her fingers experimentally and looks up.

'I did,' she says, 'but not for the reason he gave it. He was furious that I was more interested in CND demos and women's rights than learning how to run an estate. It was radical enough, for him, that I was a woman, his only child and heir. He gave me the chain to remind me who I was. And it did. It gave me courage on demos.' She gives a dry laugh, almost a cackle.

I finger the smooth mane and imagine Judith slipping out of the house dressed for a march, with the chain tucked under her shirt. There's a photo of her in the library, in ripped jeans with a placard. She's wearing a green cap with the brim pulled low over her eyes. A plait lies over her shoulder. The placard has thick black letters that say *NO!* There's an image of a mushroom cloud and the CND logo.

'You... you were a force of nature, Judith,' I tell her.

She raises her chin and looks at me. 'I stood up for what was right, that's all. Just like you do, Ruby.'

'Me?' I scoff. There's a silence. Outside there's a gust of wind which rattles the windows. Judith rocks back, pulls at the quilt and tucks it round us. I lean against the rail at the end of the bed.

'I'm a mouse, Judith,' I tell her. 'I'm not like you.' The golf ball is back. I swallow.

She leans forward and grabs me then, but the nearest body part is my foot beneath the quilt. She can't lean any further because of her back. I can't lean forward because she might see the wetness in my eyes.

'You're not a mouse!' The words come out forcefully, perhaps more so than she intended. She clears her throat, still gripping my foot. It's beginning to throb but I'm too busy with the golf ball.

Judith is swallowing. Perhaps she has a golf ball too.

'Matthew suffered from anxiety,' she says at last.

'Dad?' I'm genuinely amazed. Dad was always so laid back, so funny.

Judith nods. 'He hated boarding school. I wanted to take him away, but your grandfather wouldn't hear of it. He went to that school. That's when I gave your father the chain, to keep in his pocket.'

Dad never talked about boarding school, except to say he was unhappy. Then to tell us we were going to the local school, which made Judith cross.

'I never knew he had anxiety,' I say.

'And look what he went on to do!' Judith says. 'Travel the world, train as a psychologist, start his own practice. His experience of anxiety led him to help others. It's what he loved, and it was the making of him.'

I think of Dad's face, of the way he used to bring his eyes up really close to mine until both our eyes crossed. I think of him at work, how intently he listened when people spoke, how gentle he was, how confident, happy in his own skin.

Judith's grip on my foot tightens. Her face has changed back, and her eyes are a stab of blue.

'What do you love, Ruby?'

I look away. The golf ball is still there.

'I'd love you to let go of my foot,' I tell her.

She lets go, but carries on.

'You fight for the things that matter, Ruby. I've watched you. You know instinctively how to help. And you don't think twice, you just do it. Look at how you took charge yesterday!'

I frown. How does she know about that?

She fumbles in her dressing-gown pocket and pulls out a folded sheet of paper. She waves it at me.

'I've made a list. I went on the university website. There are so many causes you could get involved in, ways to make a difference. You should look at them.'

Slowly, I reach out and take the paper. I unfold it and see she has handwritten a list of volunteering opportunities. There are so many that the page is covered. I glimpse a few – the Green Party, the Environment Society, Amnesty International. Her writing is so small, there must be more than twenty organisations on just one side.

'It's taken you a while to do this, hasn't it?'

She lifts her chin, looks me square in the eye. 'I was going to send it to you,' she says. 'But then I thought it would be better to see you in person.'

I think of the solicitor, his awkwardness; of the strange, almost unbelievable circumstances we found ourselves in last night.

I lean forward and give her a hard stare, the sort she gives us. I ask her, but it's not really a question. 'There's no "chain" problem, is there?'

There is a beat. 'No,' she says.

The breath catches in my throat, and I swear openly.

'I can't believe you put us through that!' I'm shouting but I don't care. 'It nearly broke Mum! Why would that Steve guy say there was a problem if there wasn't?'

She has the grace to redden a bit. 'I know him and his father well. They've done some work for me in the past. He told me about the people further up the chain, and I might have meddled a bit.'

I'm panting with the shock of it, knowing what she's done. How could she?

'Look.' Judith unfolds herself and gets up, set for a fight. 'He didn't all know the details, if it's any consolation. He was just the messenger. And before you judge me, I invited you all for Christmas, but your mother declined. Do you really think she could have moved you into the new place and put together a Christmas for you, for Noah? She would never have coped, and it would have been you picking up the pieces as ever. And a decent Christmas is what you all need.'

I want to argue, to shout that it isn't true. But she's right. Mum is still grieving, struggling with daily life, so God knows how she could think of moving again so soon. I'm not even sure if she's sorted out things like the TV or internet, although I keep reminding her. And if I hadn't been around for the last few weeks, we wouldn't have even packed in time.

Judith tightens the belt of her dressing gown.

'Al is back tomorrow,' she says, 'and it's Christmas Eve. We'll go and choose a tree to cut down. You and Noah can decorate it like you used to. We'll light the fire in the drawing room, play games.'

The thought of all this is appealing and she knows it. But I'm not giving her the pleasure, not yet.

'How did you do it?' I ask her coldly. 'Offer the vendors money?'

There is another beat. 'It wasn't quite like that,' she says, her voice quiet for once. 'Steve kept me informed. There was already a problem, but it would only have delayed things a day or so. I happen to know the people involved and I just...' – she falters for a moment – '...built on what was already there.'

'When Mum finds out, she'll go crazy,' I tell her.

My grandmother shrugs. 'Does she need to know?'

I think about this for a moment. It's a lot to ask. But we both know Mum is the child in this family at the moment, and I'm not. Despite being a socially anxious teenager. How does that work?

She's about to go, but I'm curious. 'How did you know I'd suggest it, coming to you?'

She gives me a level look. 'It was the only option, and I knew you'd think of it,' she says. 'You always do, Ruby.' She nods as if dismissing a tradesman. Then she leaves.

I stand for a moment in the middle of the room. Then I put the box back under the bed. I turn out the light just as the clouds part and the moon sails into view. I lean against the wall by the door, hold the chain between my fingers, trace the lion's face. The room is still light. I see the sky through four windows, sprinkled with stars. I feel the vastness and the smallness, and I don't feel afraid.

Is Judith right? If I go back to uni and volunteer for things I care about, could I survive, find my place?

I touch the chain again, feel the words on the pendant. *Trust who you're meant to be.*

I think of taking control last night, of kicking Max when he hit Tomasz, of sticking up for Marcos with the rota.

'It could work,' I tell the moon. I fold the paper and put it in my pocket.

Inching my way down the stairs, I hold the chain with greedy fingers. Somehow, its twisted links connect me to Dad's courage, Judith's strength, her father's determination.

And despite everything, there's a frisson of hope. Because some chains can't be broken.

The Gift

'So, what did you get her for Christmas?'

Duncan responds by pushing his glasses up his nose. The stuffy heat in the council offices makes him sweat, so they spend the day joy-riding off his face. He looks in Lisa's direction. It's hard to think of her as an intern, partly because of her age (fifty?) and partly because she's better at her job than the not-interns. Which is the rest of them.

He parts the leaves of 'their plant' so he can see her. It's a peace lily but more annoying than peaceful, trapping the rest of the office behind its abundant foliage. Though this is mostly a good thing. Each pair of desk-owners was asked to select one in line with the council's Greener Desk for Well-Being policy. Duncan chose it after googling 'Plants you can't kill'. It was Number Two. He never goes for Number One on principle.

On the other side of the plant, Lisa is waiting, head on one side. Her lipstick has come off and her eyeliner (too black, too thick) has begun to liquify. She looks sort of faded – leftovers of the bright person she came to work as. But her eyes are kind, interested.

'Well…' Duncan sighs. He can't bring himself to tell her. It's Christmas Eve, after all.

Lisa's eyes widen. 'You did get her something?'

Duncan takes off his glasses. It will be better if he can't see her. 'I looked for perfume, I really did,' he says, 'but those cosmetics counters are so confusing and the saleswomen are terrifying. I couldn't bring myself to talk to them.'

'So...' says Lisa's voice with studied calm (he is thankful for space where her face should be) '...you did what I said and wandered around looking at things like scarves and gloves.'

Duncan wants to put the plant back. 'No,' he says. 'I got on the bus and went home.'

'*Duncan Greaves!*'

He puts his glasses on. She's frowning and crossing and uncrossing her arms in front of her on the desk, making her breasts wobble. Guiltily, he looks away.

'I can't believe you didn't get anything! It's Christmas *Eve*, for goodness' sake! You're going tonight, aren't you? What's she going to think?'

Duncan shrugs. He's given up anticipating his sister's reaction to gifts; she's so unpredictable. Last year he bought her a lamp, which she said was too big and too bright and clashed with everything. The year before he bought her a vase, one with raised glass leaves all over it – he thought women loved that kind of thing. But when she unwrapped it and thanked him, she gave Joanne one of the looks she often gives her when he's around. Though, to be fair, Joanne always frowns back.

He sighs. 'There's no point getting her anything,' he says. 'The two of them just...' He looks round and then remembers they're the only two left. 'They don't like me. I don't know why. Maybe they only like gays.'

'Don't be ridiculous!' Lisa says. 'Sexual orientation has nothing to do with it. You're being an old man!'

This does nothing for his mood. Being alone is bad enough, but being alone and old is even worse. 'My brother is a confirmed bachelor,' Lin tells people. It's a term he hates. As if it's something you apply for. An image swims through his mind: robe-clad officials with firm handshakes.

Duncan Greaves, I can now confirm that you are, officially, a bachelor.

But he has done it accidentally. Fallen into it like you fall into holes. It's not as though he hasn't tried. There have been women through the years: Jen said he was boring, so he grew his hair and gave up Bach. Madge said he looked unkempt and smelled of basil, so he went to the barber and stopped growing herbs. When Celia asked him what he actually did in his spare time, he panicked and said he was between interests at the moment. Would she like to suggest some? She gave him a long look and said the relationship was going nowhere. He had given up women and joined a choir. He would never forget who he was again.

The problem with women is they want to mould you into something convenient, so instead he got a cat. Then he found out Steve was one hundred per cent Steph. But by then it was too late, because he loved her. Perhaps this is what happens to most men. He just hasn't held on to a woman long enough to find out.

'I didn't mean that,' says Lisa, looking contrite. 'I was frustrated about the present. You're not much older than me, and I'm not old!'

He looks at her then. Her eyelids are hooded and there are wrinkles on her neck. Her dyed red hair and too-black brows are startling, as are her ring-clad fingers and chunky necklace. The blue beads are huge. How does she avoid whiplash? In the monochrome surroundings of the council office, she is as unexpected as a rare bird.

'It's OK,' he says, and tries to change the subject. 'Have you updated the register? If so, we can go.' On the other side of the lily, the office desks with their plants and switched-off computers have a blank look, as if surprised at being abandoned already. But most council employees drift off early on Christmas Eve. He's only there because he has nowhere to go. He isn't expected at Lin and Joanne's until seven, and as for Lisa…

'What are you doing for Christmas anyway?' he asks.

But she's still on about the present. 'Look, it's only five. If you go now, you can find something, if you're quick. Most of Henford is open until five thirty. You could try Frampton's. They have lovely stuff. Like vases,' she adds hopefully.

Duncan gets up, yawns, stretches. 'She hates vases,' he says. 'But thanks. What are you doing for Christmas, Lisa?'

'Oh, I have plans! And more importantly, I have presents, for *everyone*!' Lisa gets up and the beads somersault. Duncan winces. She stuffs her pen into an already overcrowded pen pot and rakes a pile of tangerine peel into the bin. She bends down to switch her computer off. To avoid looking at her breasts, he stares at her desk, which is covered in bits of orange pith.

His own desk, by contrast, is spotless. His pen pot holds two of each colour – black, blue and red – along with two highlighters and two staplers looped over the edge.

'Why do you need two of everything?' she had once asked him. And his response, even to himself, sounded lame.

'For back-up.'

Most people are probably too busy for back-up. Back-up is no doubt a luxury for those with empty lives.

You're a sad, lonely bachelor with nothing to look forward to. He pushes the Voice firmly away (it's somehow louder at Christmas). After all, Lin's not much younger than he is and she has no children. But she does have Joanne. He remembers when she told him, in her mid-thirties, that she was gay. It was one of those times when he misunderstood, and she laughed. But to be fair to him, she had deliberately tried to mislead him, perhaps expecting judgement. Which didn't come. How can you judge something you don't understand? And over the years, he has tried, he really has, but his questions for Lin have always come out wrong. His little sister is the prickly one, *like your mother –*

that's what Dad used to say. *You're easy-going, like me, Duncan.*
God rest their souls.

But Joanne has always been kind to him. If he's completely
honest, and he feels disloyal even thinking this, he gets on better
with her than he does with his own sister. He knows Lin loves him;
of course she does. But he also knows he is her 'boring big brother'
who works at the council, lives with his cat and has no dress sense.
No one wears brown trousers these days, Duncan! He remembers
being bewildered by this. Why does it even matter?

They make their way towards the lift. The office, beneath its
tinsel and miniature Christmas tree, is sour with disapproval. The
lift arrives. As they get in and turn towards the doors, Duncan
says, 'Henford Town Council would like to wish you all a very
Happy Christmas.' He looks down at Lisa, expecting her to smile.
She lets out a rather forced cackle.

After the office, the cold hits like a slap. They burrow into their
coats – his long and dark with a high collar, hers a patchwork
jacket with hood. They part on the high street.

'I'll be off, then,' he says. 'Half an hour until the shops shut.'

'Oh!' There's light in her eyes as she looks up at him. 'You're
going to try, then? Let me know if you find anything!'

'Happy Christmas.' He smiles into her panda eyes. Despite her
messy desk and inappropriate dress sense, she really is a lovely
person. And her spreadsheets are second to none.

She reaches up and gives him a peck on the cheek. 'Happy
Christmas, Duncan! Thanks for being so kind to a silly old intern.'
And with that she turns, hitches her huge multicoloured handbag
over her shoulder and begins to trail up the hill.

Stunned, Duncan watches her. On either side, light falls out
of shop windows onto pavements crusted with frost. A woman
cycles down the road. Someone has put tinsel on the top of the
postbox. The high street is emptying, and Lisa cuts a lonely figure,

pounding up the steepest part of the hill in her boots, head down. But there's something solid about her, something reassuring. And, after all, there's no need to pity her. She has her Christmas all wrapped up, which is more than he does.

As he turns and walks down the road towards Frampton's, it strikes him that despite her chatter and her friendly ways, he knows little about her except that she lives alone. Pity she's not his type. Is it possible she thinks he's hers? He lifts his hand and touches the remains of the kiss.

Frampton's is closed, as are Sarah's, Lavell's and even Sussex Stationers. He suddenly feels desperate. His lack of enthusiasm for Christmas this year has resulted in a kind of numb denial, disintegrating with each closed shop. He knows how much Lin loves the time of year. Just like Mum did. She spends so long planning and buying and cooking. Being a butcher helps too – the meat is always incredible. Her presents are generous and well thought-out. She insists he join them for dinner on Christmas Eve, for lamb and Mum's raspberry pavlova, and stay until Boxing Day. When he thinks about it, her love language is probably doing stuff, whereas his is saying stuff. And perhaps that's where they've been going wrong all these years. Also, with a sudden burst of clarity, it hits him that she likes useful things, practical not pretty. No wonder she hated the lamp and the vase.

The bottles of alcohol and expensive chocolates that he's been telling himself 'will be fine' suddenly seem shameful. They'll have loads of those anyway. He can't turn up without a present, he just can't. He must get her something. Anything.

Quickening his pace, he walks the length of the street, staring into shops on both sides. How can they have closed so early? *It's Christmas Eve, you idiot!* the Voice points out. Of course they're closed. The whole world has done its shopping by now.

He pauses at the corner near the council offices, out of breath. Leaning against the wall next to the hardware shop, he feels that strange trickle of winter sweat that you get when you overexert yourself in cold weather. Like being freeze-dried.

He is panting slightly from fast-walking uphill. *Hope I don't have a heart attack*, he thinks.

He sighs and glances down the street one last time. It's empty apart from a cluster of parked cars by an Indian takeaway. He turns to go.

But something catches his eye, and he turns. Through the window next to him, he can see a man in a brown overall tidying up near a till. And the shop is open.

The door tinkles when he goes in. The man looks up. He has a ruddy face and bald head.

'Hello, mate! Late gift, is it?' He laughs at his joke but stops when he sees Duncan's face. Duncan can see it too, in a mirror behind the till. It looks defeated. He nods at the man (and at his glum reflection, but at least *he* has a full head of hair).

'Well, what do you know, it is!' exclaims the man. 'Well, you've come to the right place.' He points proudly towards the Christmas window display. 'I told Bev it would be worth opening late. You've only got two minutes, mind. We've got the grandkids coming... I live in Eastleigh,' he adds, tapping his watch.

Two minutes! But it's two minutes he didn't think he'd have. Two minutes to choose a present for his sister. From a hardware shop.

He needs to climb over a few things as the floor is full of buckets and baskets that mostly sit outside. But they've not done a bad job with the display, considering people don't usually give things like spin mops for Christmas. The whole thing has been cunningly arranged with tinsel, greenery and tiny lights in all the right places. The effect is so pleasing that you're suddenly filled with longing for a pack of tea towels or a power tool.

Right on the edge, nearest the door, is a whisk tied with red ribbon. It's one of those old-fashioned ones with a handle that you turn and two whisks with large loops. It reminds him of one Mum had.

'OK!' says the hardware man, raising his arm to point at his watch. 'Time's up, mate. It's now or never.'

Duncan's neck prickles with indecision. He picks up the whisk and at that moment he has two memories. One is of young Lin, using an identical whisk to cool fudge on their mum's kitchen hob. The other is Joanne telling him how annoying Lin is, preferring useful presents to expensive ones.

Hardware Man leans against the till holding his keys. 'That's a sterling whisk, that is,' he says. 'A Vintage Victoria 2000. Bargain at the price.'

Duncan can tell he wants to be on his way. Off to his wife and grandkids. Let Christmas begin in Eastleigh...

He buys it.

Her flat is at the end of a narrow lane at the top of the hill. He inches his way across the cobbles, careful not to slip on the ice. The block is at the end and the road badly lit. He has his briefcase in one hand and the whisk in the other, so can't use his phone torch to help him. Eventually, with faltering steps, he reaches the one light by the door. A woman is coming out holding a bunch of flowers and a baby. He holds the door for her while she edges around it awkwardly. At one point, the baby's face is so close, all he can see are eyes – perfect circles – and a fist-filled mouth full of dribble. As they squeeze past, the baby takes out its fists and gives him a dazzling smile. Something inside him jumps. The woman thanks him and wishes him a happy Christmas. He turns and watches them as they walk towards their car, but the baby has lost interest and is reaching its gummy hands towards her face. He goes through into the hall and climbs the stairs. Next to the doorbell, behind a strip of plastic, is her name written in tidy writing.

When she answers the door, he holds up the whisk sheepishly.

'I panicked,' he says.

Lisa's surprised eyes move from his face to the whisk and then – and this is unexpected – they both burst out laughing. They laugh so hard that he forgets to breathe and must pant in big gasping breaths to reoxygenate. She leans against the doorframe and clutches her stomach with ring-clad fingers. Her red hair has been gathered into an untidy bunch on top of her head and flips as she shakes. A couple of doors open nearby.

Lisa regains control. 'I think you'd better come in,' she wheezes.

They carry on laughing in the tiny hall and he leans against the wall for support. Through a half-open door, he has a glimpse of presents laid out beneath a tree. They are beautifully wrapped in paper and real ribbon.

Eventually they get a grip and stand for a moment panting like runners.

'I don't know why that was so funny,' Duncan says, wiping his eyes.

'Me neither.' Lisa smiles up at him. 'But I'm glad you came to show me. It may be my best moment all Christmas!'

'Really?' He glances through the door to the presents and wonders what she means. Lisa puts a hand to her face, which is beginning to flush.

'Why don't you come in?' she says. 'I've got an idea.' She reaches for the whisk, and he gives it to her.

She pushes the inner door open, and he walks into a small room. In the corner is a TV on which the film *The Sound of Music* is playing. Next to the window is a tree intended for use in a much bigger room. It's so tall the top is bent against the ceiling. Piles of presents have been carefully arranged beneath it, along with tiny lights and greenery. The tree's own lights blink on and off, changing colour each time, the effect slightly dizzying. The curtains are open and there's an impressive view across the town, a Jenga of yellow strips sliding into darkness, some laced and strung for Christmas. On the table is an open bottle of champagne and two glasses.

Now that they've stopped laughing and are here together, on non-office territory, awkwardness hits. They usually talk about work things, or other things when they should be working. Here, their interactions are out of sync, their shape unknown.

Duncan clears his throat. 'Great view!' he says, and then points to the glasses. 'Guest arriving?'

Lisa is busying herself with the whisk. The flush is creeping towards her neck.

'Er, she was, but not now. Would you join me,' she says, 'while I execute my idea?'

Duncan is confused. Who would pull out last minute, on Christmas Eve? Or is she one of those deluded people who pretend someone is with them when they're not? He saw one in a café once, having a full conversation over coffee with nothing but fresh air. He had been filled with compassion, so much so that he'd said 'Excuse me,' when edging past said Fresh Air towards the door. It was like the Emperor's New Clothes.

He looks at his watch. It's only ten to six.

'OK.' He sits down on a corner chair so stuffed with cushions there's no room for a backside. She hands him a glass and they toast each other with a tiny, embarrassed jerk of the glasses in the other's direction. Her eyes are full of something, but he can't decide what.

'Happy Christmas!' they say with gusto.

There is a small hesitation and then, as if making up her mind, Lisa says, 'I won't be a mo.'

She puts her glass down and bends to pick up a present from under the tree. Her sleeve rides up and he can see, on her arms, scars. The present is rectangular and decorated with an elaborate bow.

While she is scuffling in the other room – it must be the bedroom as the flat doesn't seem big enough for much else – he begins to feel more and more uneasy. After all, what does he really know about Lisa Goodwood? She was taken on via the internship scheme, the government's attempt to get folk back to work. She was very quiet for the first couple of months, but her efficiency was impressive, and he had found he could rely on her for more and more of the day-to-day running of things. He knew she lived in social housing because he had delivered a file to her one weekend and had been impressed at the loveliness of the block: new but fitting in with the older houses on the hill.

At work, little by little, he managed to draw her out; the others followed his lead and she, over time, thawed. As his workload increased, her desk was moved next to his. They now have a good working relationship and satisfying banter. She is effectively his PA, which allows him to impress as never before and, as number two in Waste Handling and Management, to feel more confident when deputising for his boss. Without her, he would never have had the courage to promote the idea of a council recycling stall at the local music festival. What a roaring success that had been, raising his status considerably at the council. Especially as this was where he had met Judith Trenton, a local landowner, whose friendship has resulted in several benefits as the years have gone by. Procuring such a generous and influential patron was something the boss could boast about. And all this because of Lisa.

No wonder he's allowed her glimpses into his life not permitted to others, including the 'What shall I get my sister for Christmas?' thing.

But, lovely as she is, she's too zany for him, and she's a woman. He has tried them before, and it didn't end well. He's can't risk it again. *Why did you come here, then?* He has a too-large swig of champagne and pushes the Voice aside. What is she doing in the other room? Unwrapping a present so she can wrap the whisk for him? Does she think he has no paper at home? Has she judged her own wrapping paper so exactly? He thinks of the seven unused rolls at the bottom of his wardrobe. Unlikely.

He's about to call through, to explain he has giftwrap at home, to tell her not to trouble herself, when she reappears, red and breathless in the doorway. Some of her hair has escaped and is curling in front of her face. She blows it aside. A box is brandished in his direction.

'What do you think?'

It's a double-sized shoebox, carefully wrapped and decorated with ribbon. She lifts the lid, which is wrapped in matching paper. Inside the box, she has artfully arranged a sort of vintage collection of kitchen things – one of those old-fashioned egg timers, a butter dish, a wooden chopping board and the whisk. She has an eye for detail and the box set, with its sprig of holly, ribbon and Christmassy tissue paper, makes you wonder how you've lived without it.

He's blown away, but of course he can't accept it.

'Lisa,' he says, 'I... I...'

She cannot hide her desperation. 'Please,' she says. 'OK, so I bought them for myself and wrapped them, just in case...' She tails off. 'I love stuff like this. You can pay me if it makes you feel better, but let me do this. Please.'

She pushes the box into his arms and reaches for her glass.

Duncan's emotions are so conflicted he feels dizzy. Is he to understand she's wrapped up a present to open herself and is now giving it to him?

He feels very awkward, and his impulse is to get away as fast as he can. He thought he would show her the whisk, they'd have a giggle and then he'd go to Lin's. But something else is going on here. It's not really about the present.

'I thought... I thought...' His mouth tries to say things but stops because he doesn't know what they should be.

Lisa sinks into the other chair, which is also stuffed with cushions. She reaches behind her and throws a few off with more vehemence than needed. She glugs champagne, then puts the glass down. She tips forward and puts her head in her hands. The words, from between her fingers, are muffled.

'Look, Duncan, you don't know much about me, but I'm not the person you think. I... I've been in prison...'

Her words tail away. Duncan is horrified. 'Look, Lisa, you don't need to...'

Things are bad, he thinks, when neither of them can finish sentences.

'No, I... I want to,' she says. 'I want to explain.' She gives an enormous sigh. 'I was in a coercive relationship, and didn't know I was taking drugs to people. I was naive and desperate and... hungry. The boss knew, obviously, when he employed me, but I didn't want others to know. It's bad enough as it is.'

In the silence that follows, Duncan can hear a burst of music from another flat. Someone is having a party. A world away from this poor woman's life with her overdecorated tree and self-bought presents. Before he's decided what to feel – horror or compassion – Lisa continues.

'My daughter has refused to see me. Things went wrong there. But sometimes she turns up unexpectedly and I... I've prepared, just in case.' The way she speaks is humbling. Her voice is quiet, desperate, but not out of control like when they were laughing. This is a long sadness.

'She still might come,' she whispers, 'but I thought I'd buy myself some treats just in case. Why not?' She looks up defensively at this point and sits back on the chair. Her face is wet and her eyeliner, already smudged, is pooling beneath her eyes. She makes no attempt to wipe it. *It is what it is*, thinks Duncan. He has rarely experienced such extremes of emotion. He has an urge to escape, but his heart is breaking.

She pushes hair out of her eyes and blows her nose. 'I have a lot to celebrate, actually,' she tells him, tossing her head. 'I've turned my life around and, whether you know it or not, you've been a big part of that, Duncan.'

She gives him a watery smile. 'It would give me so much pleasure if you'd take this, for your sister.'

And there it is. His get-out. Filled with shame at his cowardice, he nevertheless stands, clutching the present.

'Then I will,' he hears himself saying. 'Thank you, Lisa. I'll pay you in the New Year. And I hope, I really do' – at this point he looks into her eyes and trusts he's communicating his strength of feeling here – 'that she comes, your daughter.'

Lisa nods. She stands too and, hesitantly, they make their way into the hall.

As he leaves, he turns guiltily towards her. 'If she doesn't come,' he says, 'will you... will you be alright, tomorrow?'

'Of course!' she says. 'I'm in my own place, warm, cosy, with food and presents. I can watch what I want on telly. I'll be in heaven!'

But her answer is too quick, too bright. And they both know it.

Lin opens the door in her butcher's garb. As usual her apron is spattered with cooking and something he hopes very much isn't blood. Although blood is what he feels he deserves. But what else could he have done?

'Wow, what a present!' She stares wonderingly at Lisa's tastefully wrapped box and ushers him into the hall. Here, the ghosts of his parents hover among the mirrors and rugs, which haven't changed since his youth. Lin and Joanne have kept things as they were.

In his parents' lounge, the fire has been lit and the tree, covered in baubles and strung with white lights, whispers a welcome. Lin bends to put his gift next to the others, her ample arms stretching to achieve the most pleasing angle. He pushes an image of Lisa's scars away. Lin crawls back out and gets up. She turns with a smile.

'Why so glum, Duncan? It's Christmas!' She grabs him and whirls him round, tossing her head and dislodging his glasses. He pulls himself away and grabs them before they fall. She laughs.

'Sorry, Duncan! Cheer up. Joanne's doing cocktails!'

On the old sideboard, where his mum served sherry, Joanne is mixing drinks. He gives her an awkward hug.

She greets him warmly while Lin disappears into the kitchen. There is a smell of lamb, and, through the door, the soaring sound of carols.

'Good day? Did you knock off early?' Joanne asks, offering him a drink. He points towards a bottle of red. But before he can answer, there's a fizz, a thump and expletives from the kitchen. Joanne gives a start. He rolls his eyes. *Welcome to Christmas with my sister.* You can never anticipate the mood change.

Before Joanne can reach the door, Lin is there, holding a twist of metal. Her apron is covered in crud, and she looks like thunder.

Duncan picks up the glass Joanne poured and takes a mouthful. The red wine is bitter after the champagne. He's trying very hard to concentrate on the here and now, not to think about Lisa. But the here and now isn't exactly encouraging him to keep a stake in it. He needs another drink but is feeing light-headed. He puts the glass down.

They stand there, the three of them, until cream begins to drip on the carpet.

Lin reverses at speed, swearing. Duncan rolls his eyes. He hopes Mum is somewhere where she can't hear.

'What is that,' he asks Joanne, 'some kind of mixer?'

She's already on her hands and knees, soaking up the splodges with a tissue. 'It's an electric whisk,' she says. 'The pavlova's stuffed now. And so, probably, is Christmas. You know what she's like.' She sighs.

But Duncan is under the tree. This is his moment.

When Lin has been persuaded that it's OK to open the present now – she's almost incapable of breaking a tradition – and he's been hugged and cried over and generally the cause of far too much emotion, she beats the cream for the pavlova, and they sit down to eat.

'I just can't get over it!' she says. 'I love vintage stuff! They're the same things Mum had years ago. How clever of you, Duncan!'

He opens his mouth to tell her that it wasn't really him, but no words come. She's right, though. Away from the box, the egg timer, butter dish and chopping board, as well as the whisk, are as familiar as old friends. He is glad for Lin. He should have realised long ago that these things make her happy.

The carols have come to an end. The rich tones of Sinatra ring out.

'What a great way to start Christmas!' Lin chortles. Her eyes are glowing and so is her face. 'You've saved the day, Duncan. I owe you big time. Tell me what I can do for you. Anything!' She waves her cake fork grandly; relief makes her generous.

Duncan thinks of a hand with too many rings, and a scarred arm. He thinks of unwrapping gifts you've wrapped yourself, of how you'd look up every time you heard a noise, of how hope dies: slowly.

He doesn't know whether it's the whisk or the wine or the way the candles flicker on Lin's face, making her look so much more palatable than usual. But to his surprise, he hears his voice above the music. And it sounds like someone else's – clear, decisive.

'You can invite someone to lunch.' He forks some pavlova into his mouth.

Lin looks at Joanne and raises her eyebrows.

'Sure!' she replies. 'Whenever you like.'

Duncan swallows a raspberry. There's a burst of sweetness on his tongue.

'Tomorrow,' he says.

Something for Yourself

A woman drives through woods in winter. On either side of the car, trees stand tall and sulk, resenting how winter lingers at the year's turn. The woman is scared. She is the fifth carer for the old man, and no one has told her why. But she's heard the stories and she is afraid.

It's New Year's Eve but that makes no difference to the woman. Her sons are at work; her husband sleeps. There is no party for her. Amy and Kim offered to bring wine round but, as ever, she pushed them away. What's the point? It's another year. There is nothing to celebrate.

She is getting older; they all are. But her life has grown small, shrunk to the size of the labels she wears – nurse, carer, cleaner. Recipient of Universal Credit. At home, she feels trapped; in the street, invisible. No one looks at her. There is nothing remarkable about old people. She has signed her name on so many forms, so how come she's forgotten who she is?

The light is dying, and the road ahead narrows and fades. In spring this piece of woodland is covered with flowers, but in winter it feels barren, brooding. She turns on the headlights, and slows to avoid potholes and fallen branches. The trees shoulder together, thick as thieves. A deer darts out in front of the car. The woman is mesmerised by its velvet-eyed grace, almost forgetting to stop. But she is going slowly, and instinct takes over. They pause, nose to bonnet, and the woman sees briefly in its face the same fear as on her own. Then it's gone, swift and slender, a flit between trees.

The car lurches on until the road itself ends, a footpath disappearing into the forest. The woman had been warned of this.

'Are you sure?'

Her boss, Maureen, had narrowed her eyes, looked her up and down with a doubtful face. 'It's very isolated, the cabin. You'll have to walk for ten minutes in darkness once the road ends. That's why no one will do evenings.'

The woman had nodded. But it was only a half-hour drive away, not far from Ashdown House where she cleans twice a week. Better pay, too (double for awkwardness, triple for New Year). Apparently, the latest carer threw in the towel just before Christmas. Maureen coped but wanted a regular now.

'I'll take it,' she had replied. What else would she be doing on New Year's Eve?

Now, she stops the car, gathers her things, gets out. As an afterthought, she leans in and puts the interior light on so she will see it on her return. When she slams the door, there's a fluttering, a rustling. It makes her jump. She stands there for a moment, thinking of the hidden life around her, barely perceptible in the grass and trees: mice, foxes, owls. *I should live in a forest*, she thinks, picking up her bag and torch. She breathes in the scent of soil and dampness, strangely energised. The cast of other people's worries – her mother's health, her husband's gloom – always processing through her head clump to a halt. As if from a distance, she observes them, puzzled, unused to their silence. Then she switches on her torch and marches towards the path.

The torch is very powerful. 'Don't look at it, ever!' Maureen had barked. 'It will literally blind you.'

So she holds the bulky gadget carefully pointing away, its mighty eye picking out every twist and turn in the path ahead.

She avoids mud, steps over roots. She likes the sound of her feet swishing against the long grass. Strange that at home, in the light, she feels as though she's falling, heavy with the sadness of those she loves. But here, alone in the dark, with the light of a single torch, she strides ahead, confident. Her legs feel strong, her sixty-year-old body supple. She could walk forever.

At last, she sees a light. She stops, turns off her torch. It's only a pinprick, but the tiniest light offers hope for a journey's end. She switches on the torch again and points it down. The glimmer ahead grows bigger. She can make it out now: a lantern strung on a branch; behind, a wooden cabin. She has arrived.

She hesitates briefly outside the sturdy building, then knocks on wood that, even in the darkness, she can see has weathered to the colour of trees. A snuffling sound comes from the other side of the door, and the low drone of a radio, music.

'Hello?' she calls. The word repeats itself, bounding and rebounding through the woods. The snuffling becomes louder, accompanied by a series of small barks. A dog. Maureen did not mention a dog.

There is a banging and scraping as if someone is struggling to get to the door. It swings open. And there he is, the 'woodland giant'. He is indeed tall – the crutch he is leaning on is far too short and he looks bent over, uncomfortable. He glares up at her with hostile eyes partly obscured by wild eyebrows. At his feet bounces an eager terrier. He springs forward, barks and licks her hand. The woman smiles. She leans down and fondles his neck.

'Hello!' she says warmly. 'They didn't tell me about you!'

The old man snorts. 'You're useless, you are,' he tells the dog. 'You're supposed to protect me from strangers, not befriend them.'

The dog looks up at him, head on one side. The old man har-rumphs but the woman sees a change, a softening. He turns and clumps back towards his chair by the hearth.

'You'd better come in,' he calls over his shoulder.

So she does, closing the door, putting down her things, removing her coat. The dog snuffles at her bag and torch with a curious nose. She hangs her coat on a hook near the door and looks around. It's an Aladdin's cave.

There are leather chairs, lamps, a wood-burning stove; books line every wall. The surfaces of a large table and antique desk are covered with papers, the wood floor strewn with rugs. This must be murder for a man on crutches, but their colourful threads make the room sing. A kitchen area to the right of the door boasts a wooden worktop, Aga and red-tiled floor. Everywhere there are wooden carvings, some clearly fashioned for a purpose – a scoop chair, a stool, a set of bowls – others decorative. There is a cat, a mouse, a reindeer. And next to the fire, a beautiful branch, smooth and polished to a shine.

The old man has retreated to an upright chair on the other side of the fire, and is painfully hoisting his leg onto a stool. Behind him, a half-open door reveals a lattice window, the corner of a bed.

The woman is enchanted. 'What a beautiful house!'

'You think?' The old man sniffs. He bangs his walking stick on the ground so suddenly that the woman jumps. The dog, now curled in front of the fire, doesn't flinch. 'It's a savage place to live when you can't walk!' he shouts, voice rising with each word. His accent is Irish, his voice gravel.

The woman is still. There's a sigh from the dog, a hiss from the fire. But beyond the house, in the air between trees, stretching for miles in every direction, silence. The old man glances at her from beneath shaggy eyebrows. His expression is curious. She picks up her bag and takes out a clipboard, latex gloves.

'So will I help with the leg?' she says.

He roars again but this time she is ready and, like the dog, doesn't flinch.

'I don't want your help!' His vehemence makes him cough, which at least diffuses things. She moves swiftly to the sink and pours a glass of water. By the time she's placed it on the table near him, his face is purple and his eyes are streaming. He picks up the glass, his body shuddering with the effort of not coughing. He drinks greedily.

She pulls a chair over to where he's sitting and waits, quietly, next to the leg. After a while, he recovers.

'Well, you're a funny one,' he says. 'Most of them would have left by now.'

She gives him a steady look. 'It'll take more than that to scare me off,' she says. 'I'm used to awkward men. I'm married to one.'

At this, he throws back his head and laughs. The skin on his chin, beneath his beard, is red and tight. 'You're Irish, aren't you?' he says. 'Not much of an accent left but I can tell. It explains your stubbornness.'

Truce. She smiles. A stillness. They are quietly assessing each other for possibilities. A log spits. Somewhere outside there's a call. She tilts her head, listens.

'Is that an owl?'

'It is.' He sighs and begins to roll up his trouser leg.

'I didn't think they hooted in winter.' She actually has no idea. She's just trying to keep the wolf (his temper) from the door (her job).

He has finished rolling up his trousers. The wound gapes redly from beneath the bloodied bandage. He allows himself a small breath. He looks at her.

'You clearly don't know much about owls, then.'

Calmly, she begins to take what she needs out of the bag. 'You're right,' she says, placing her things on the rustic table between them – antiseptic, tweezers, a fresh bandage, a tub. She pulls on the gloves and sets, gently, to work.

'I was feigning an interest to stop you shouting,' she says.

This time his laugh is less hearty. He is gripping the flesh of his leg either side of the wound with both hands. His face has paled.

'You have so many books,' she says as she works. 'What do you like to read?'

'Everything,' he mutters through clenched teeth.

'Me too.'

She pauses in her efforts to peel away the congealed bandage. 'Are you alright?' she says.

He's gripping his leg so hard that the flesh has changed colour. She wants to tell him to stop but can see he's struggling to keep control.

'It's for mating,' he tells her.

'I'm sorry?' The bandage is coming off but pulling at the wound. She is slow, as gentle as possible. His reply is delivered between gritted teeth. But now his voice is so soft she must strain to hear him.

'Part of the reason they call at night is to attract a mate.' She can feel his glance, but she's looking down, with a frown of concentration. 'You and I don't need one of those, I'm guessing,' he adds, 'since the wife's warm in her grave and you have an awkward one at home.'

She looks up, as he knows she will. Their faces are close. His eyes are intelligent, brown-flecked green, young eyes in old skin of the softest leather. She pulls the last of the bandage away and dumps it in the tub along with the gloves. She pauses for a moment, looks into the fire. The flames leap and twist.

'I'm sorry,' she says, 'about your wife.'

He nods. She looks around. The room smells of woodsmoke and books. The carved footstool, the rough-hewn table and chairs make her think of a hobbit house. Simple, almost child-like, the pieces have pleasing lines and gleaming surfaces that ask to be touched.

'You're a carpenter,' she says.

'I am.' He sighs. 'That's what got me into trouble.' He jerks his head in the direction of the leg. She begins slowly to clean the wound, pretending to ignore his wince.

'I've never hurt myself cutting it up for the burner, but this…' He picks up a piece of wood from the other side of the chair. 'This is what finished me.'

The woman puts a piece of bloodied gauze in the tub and pauses, a fresh piece at the ready. Her eyes follow the piece of wood as he lifts it closer for inspection. It's an almost complete circle of wood, still rough, weathered by the elements, rings and whorls thrown liberally across its width. The top right side is cut on a diagonal, straightening the curve. The upper part of the diagonal is stained. It looks as though someone has tried to scrub it.

The woman looks closer. 'Is that blood?'

'Yes, it's blood,' he grunts, '*my* blood. My very own. Talk about blood, sweat and tears for your trade…'

'How did you do it?' She's nearly finished. She tapes the new dressing in place, around the edge of the wound.

'Like a fool, I didn't line it up properly on the bench and it slipped. I sliced a vein.' He puts the wooden circle on his knee and slumps his head, eyes lowered towards his leg. 'They say they can treat the wound, but there's permanent damage to the blood supply. I'll be disabled for life.' A sigh. '"Old, disabled man living off-grid." Doesn't sound great, does it?'

She stands and picks up the tub, pulling out a bag for surgical waste with her other hand. Tipping everything in, she takes it into the kitchen area, locates the bin, lifts the lid. As she peels off her gloves and dumps them into her bag, she wonders why such a terrible thing, like the loss of a lover, doesn't stop life hitting you with more.

She walks back to the chair, sits by the fire. The flames leap and twist; the clock strikes nine. She imagines looking down at the forest, a bird's-eye view, seeing the spread of it, the criss-cross of paths, the belts of trees, then homing in on the cabin, with its pitched roof nestled beyond the road. Down, down, inside so you could see the tops of their heads, hers and his, looking into the fire, each holding a sorrow so sharp it slices them in two.

The dog yawns and stretches. Carefully, the old man puts the wooden circle back in its place. He leans down and opens the wood burner, chucks in a log. She sees his stubborn jaw, the strong, precise movements of his hands. This is not a man used to depending on others.

The fire roars. He shuts the door. She watches the colours change behind the glass – red, blue, yellow, orange. They transform the room. Again, she thinks of the light, how in winter we are drawn to it, like moths.

'My husband has dementia.' He turns his head, watching her. She is as surprised by this revelation as he is. 'It's early on, but his father died of it and the outlook's not good.'

He nods, leans down, scratches the skin above the wound. She starts to speak but he lifts his hands and begins to roll his trouser leg down.

'How come you're here, then?' He sounds interested rather than nosy.

She holds her sigh inside, like a prayer. But perhaps he sees it. Those in pain can do that.

'He's mainly depressed right now,' she says, 'because of the diagnosis. He sleeps a lot. I can leave him for a few hours, for the caring and cleaning, until I can't do them any more.'

He nods, picking at some loose threads in his sweater. He has big, square fingers.

'He doesn't talk much now. He just wants to sleep and watch police dramas,' she tells the old man. 'The bloodier, the better. I've tried so hard to get him to come out, to do the things we love – walking, going to new places – but he won't. He says there's no point.'

'Well, I can see what he means,' he replies, shrugging. 'He won't remember them, will he?'

She stares at him, annoyed. 'Whose side are you on?'

He spreads his hands. In the background, the fridge starts to hum. 'I'm just saying, is all. That's what he's probably thinking.'

'How do you know?' The silence is short, but it splits itself open, and she sees it.

'That's how your wife died. Of dementia.' It's not a question.

Outside, there's a whisper in the trees. On the roof, the drumming of rain. The dog raises its head and scratches itself under the chin. It fixes its eyes on her reproachfully. *Don't go there*, the look says.

But he continues, his voice neutral though his feelings can't be.

'We bought the land for this place from Lady Trenton at Ashdown House.' He looks into the flames, his face turned away. 'And then we built it, piece by piece, while we huddled together in a caravan under the trees.'

He breaks off to drag a wrinkled hand across his eyes, but his voice remains quiet, controlled.

'It was built on the soil of our dreams. Five years for a dream she couldn't enjoy. Cruel, huh?'

She tries not to think of the tragedy that awaits us all, and those we love, the end of things. The effort of this almost undoes her. She needs to go, to get out.

Frantically, she begins to tidy her supplies away. But they don't seem to fit in the bag any more. She pushes, straining the canvas sides, miscalculating their width. To her alarm, her vision is blurred. Blindly, she shoves a roll of bandage into the bulging pocket.

'You didn't tell me your name,' he says.

She cannot look at him, cannot speak. But he's determined.

'The agency normally tells me,' he continues, 'but they forgot this time. Your name is...?'

She can push down pain – her particular art form – but it clambers back, gathers in her throat. She tries to swallow it, to answer. She manages to whisper her name.

'Don't cry, Jan.' His voice is very soft, very gentle. She cannot look at him. She tries valiantly to swallow, to still her trembling hands. Her heart knocks with the effort.

'It will pass,' he continues. How can this be the same man, the angry, violent man who no one will care for? 'You go with it, what he wants for what he has left. But you keep some of life for yourself – your work, your friends, your passions.' He gestures around the room, to his carved creations, his books.

She nods weakly. Mainly so she can take a breath.

'Do you hear me, Jan?' He leans forward and takes her by the arm, almost roughly, makes her look at him.

His eyes are aflame. She knows hers will be stained with tears and mascara. 'Keep some of life for yourself!'

She wipes her face with her sleeve, nods again. He lets go.

She gets up, walks unsteadily towards the door, puts on her coat. He watches her.

She puts on her gloves, her beret, turns. She wipes her face again.

'And let people help you,' he adds, watching her. 'Lady Trenton, she's been good to me. And though it goes against the grain, I've let her.'

It doesn't surprise Jan that Judith Trenton has helped him. She has helped her too, with the cleaning job and the hours, which Jan can fit in around her caring role.

'Thank you,' she says.

'You're thanking me?' He guffaws. 'You've just changed my dressing! I'll see you tomorrow. If you're good, I'll show you my books.'

He winks. She gives a weak smile, reaches for the door.

'Goodbye. Take care,' she says.

'Happy New Year,' he calls as she closes the door.

Happy New Year. It won't be happy for Tom. But she thinks of his face when she enters the room, the blank expression lit with pleasure; the reaching out with unsteady hands. There are still things in life to cherish.

She wonders if the faith of a lifetime – which she'd seen in the lusty singing of carols, word-perfect – will help him in the months to come. There is this hope.

The torch throws the path ahead into sharp relief. The rain has stopped but the wind is strong. As she plunges towards the car, the trees raise their voice to a shout. She thinks of Mike (how dare they call him the woodland giant), how broken he must have been, how brave. *Keep some of life for yourself, your friends, your passions... Do you hear me?*

She switches off the torch and stands for a moment in the wind, feels the chill of it, the pull. Around her, the winter forest moans and shakes. Yet in the next few months, beneath her feet, tiny fists will unclench – snowdrops, bluebells, gorse: the stubborn hope of the earth.

She takes a few steps, glances at her watch. The luminous hands inform her it's not yet ten. Perhaps she'll message the girls after all. Amy will be home waiting up for her daughter, Kim watching TV while her husband paints.

Looking up, she sees a dot of light, hovering between branches, the one from her car. It's only a pinprick, but the tiniest light offers hope for a journey's end.

Jan marches towards it.

Slowly Then All at Once

Judith stands on a rise near the woods. Night will soon be gone. There are no stars, and a clinging mist swirls and drifts between trees. She pulls her coat close. From here she can admire the outline of the house below. She likes how light from the main door spills into the darkness and the lamps on the drive seem small but cheering, fading as the sky pales. She holds herself very still, watching for dawn.

Light has always been a fascination – a fire, a candle, a shaft of sun from a dour sky. Sunsets, stars, lanterns, a lamp in a window. They make her stop, look again, listen. And always, they have something to tell her.

When she was a child in India, she and her family were invited to a Hindu fire-walking ceremony. Believers walked with bare feet across embers in devotion to Draupadi and to receive a blessing. Judith remembers how her mother shielded her eyes, whispering for Judith to do the same. But she could not look away. It was night and the fiery coals strewn across the worshippers' path had held her gaze like jewels.

Not long after, her obsession with dawn had begun. The moment when light comes, when night turns to day – when is it exactly? She pestered her parents and her governess until they ran out of patience.

'It's just not possible to know!' her father told her. 'If you don't believe us, get up early and see for yourself!'

So she did. Not every morning but every few days. She thought herself the original dawn hunter, searching for magic. One day she would see it, catch it, hold it in her heart like a promise. But the hazy dawns of India were not ideal for chasing the day.

Then her grandfather died, and the family travelled across the sea to England so her father could take his place as Lord Trenton. They moved into the mansion where he'd been brought up. Ashdown House was large and cold, and in the middle of nowhere. At first, Judith hated it, but then she discovered something precious. The best place to search for that crossover moment was the leaden light of an English dawn.

In winter, light comes slowly then all at once. There's a pause before night's end, an intake of breath, as if the world is unsure of doing it again. Sometimes it tricks her into thinking it won't. But it always does. The future, for a second, hangs in the balance. Then the sky shifts and pulls like a tightened face while pale fists punch the horizon. Then candy-coloured ink bleeds upwards until black turns blue and the page is turned. Today, a new page, a new book.

She misses it again; of course she does. But it hardly matters. She realised a while ago she's been chasing the wrong thing. Looking back, it's not the dawn she remembers but the part after – running down to the house to embrace her husband and child, a smile just for her, small arms around her neck. The biggest tragedy of our lives? We don't value what we have until it's gone.

Judith gives herself a shake. It's New Year's Day; she refuses to be sad.

Another year. Incredible that they keep coming, keep renewing themselves from the ashes of old ones. At times, it's unrelenting, at others a gift. The sky bleaches and it occurs to her again that winter light, in all its forms, is the most beautiful of all.

It will be a busy day, so she savours the stillness. She looks up. A star lingers, a bird calls. In the undergrowth behind her, a rustling.

She looks down at the place she has called home for over seventy years. Within those walls, she has loved and lost. She pushes this thought away too and summons a new one. She will spend this day with people she loves, in the place she loves. At eighty-five, who could want more?

There is the sound of a car and Ram's little van emerges from the top of the drive, weaving a bit. It crunches to a halt, parked at an angle. She smiles. Hardly surprising that her old friend is the first to arrive. He will be eager to make the day a success for her. His eyes had shone when she asked him if they would do a curry party, on New Year's Day.

'Of course we will, madam!' She reminds him endlessly to call her Judith, but it makes no difference. 'We will provide the kind of spread your father would have offered British dignitaries!'

At that point he had rubbed his hands together, eyes aglow. The mention of her father made her swallow. A memory. Ram at eight, his face etched with terror after witnessing the bloody death of his parents by neighbours they trusted. Such were the horrors of Partition, the seemingly random lines drawn between communities, friends, even family. Ram's father, their head gardener, gone. Ram's brothers, much older but equally helpless, thrust into grief and longing – all of them were admitted to her father's circle of care. Because when you were British you had power. When you were 'Embassy' you had more. The boys came to England with the Trentons and her father had helped them set up the first Indian restaurant in Henford. Not many Brits were as caring towards the suffering, some even adding to it. To this day, she is proud of her father for doing what he could.

She is pulled back to the present by the slam of the van door and the sight of dear Alan, fully dressed in his butler's uniform, crunching across the drive to greet Ram. She can't hear the men's words from here but watches the shouting and back-slapping with affection. They chat for a while and Ram throws his arms wide, a gesture of warmth and gratitude. Al nods and they both glance around and up. She moves behind a tree, stumbling on a hump covered in moss. She's not ready, not quite. But she will go down soon. It's cold and there's much to be done.

Ram turns to the car, opens the door. They begin to take out trays full of large foil containers and carry them towards the kitchen. She hopes Rosie will come soon. The minute she thinks this, her friend's tiny Fiat roars up the drive. It parks next to the van and the doors open. Out tumbles Tyler, clutching a toy plane. He looks around and shouts with glee. Then he runs across the gravel with it.

'Tyler, don't go far!' Rosie calls, unclipping the crying baby from her car seat and lifting her out.

Judith steps stiffly down the path and makes her way across the lawn. When Rosie sees her, she gives a cry of pleasure.

Judith is pleased, seeing how well the girl looks. Who would have thought she could improve so soon?

'I've missed you so much!' Rosie is trying to dislodge a wet fist from her cheek.

'When did Jack leave?' asks Judith, hugging her.

Rosie pushes the hair from her face and looks around vaguely for Tyler.

'Wednesday,' she says. 'I hated him going, but he was lucky to be back for Christmas. Some of them have been on the rig for weeks.'

Judith takes the baby so Rosie can open the boot. She lifts out a box she has brought from the café and hoists it to her hip.

Judith bounces the baby a little. She is proud of her friend. 'Elsie's getting such a big girl now and clearly thriving! You've done so well,' she says. 'Post-natal depression is a killer. I'm so pleased you're at the café less, too.'

They make their way towards the kitchen door. The baby is leaning over, trying to suck Rosie's cheek. She turns her head away, laughing. 'I'd like to get someone else in long-term,' she says. 'I want to start cooking again.'

Judith thinks of her years of visits to the Olive Tree, how her friend's cheerful welcome had faded, how pale she became.

'I'd never have made it without you,' Rosie tells her. 'It was killing me, all of it.'

She swings around and calls for Tyler, who bolts out of a clump of hydrangeas. They both jump. He flies past his mum to Judith and throws his arms around her waist. It's all she can do not to fall over.

'Hello, Aunty Judith, I've missed you! And your garden is just right for my glider plane...' He unwraps himself and runs around them in circles, plane held high. Judith can feel her face softening. He reminds her so much of Matthew. Is this partly why she went out of her way for the family? She hopes it was more than that.

The kitchen door flies open, and Ruby comes out. Her hair is roughly plaited, her eyes heavy.

'Sorry, Judith,' her granddaughter says with a yawn. Her eyes brighten as she sees the baby. She opens her arms. 'Is this Elsie? Hello, little one! Come and meet Noah.'

The baby goes to her, and Judith is relieved. Rosie won't enjoy the day if she's worrying about the children.

'You're so good to help today,' she tells Rosie as the baby is borne away. 'I'll keep an eye on Tyler.'

'Oh, he'll be fine out there,' says Rosie, as they go through to the kitchen. 'Especially if Noah joins in. And it's so much easier now he can hear.'

She puts her box on the table where Ram and Al are hard at work. They show her what they've done while Judith stands near the Aga holding out her hands. Warmth spreads through her, not just from the fire. She watches Rosie laughing with Ram as she puts on her apron and ties her hair. She smiles at the distant sound of Ruby and Noah's voices, playing peek-a-boo somewhere with the baby.

Al is chopping tomatoes. He looks up and their eyes meet. He knows how much today means to Judith. And she knows they will both be thinking this: it's how the kitchen should look, its immense table covered with food; people they love and more to come; an atmosphere of celebration, anticipation. He continues to chop, the tiniest tremble in those practised hands. She is filled with affection for this man, who has stayed by her side these past years, not a butler so much as a loyal friend and companion. Would she still be here if it wasn't for Alan?

Judith slips off her coat and takes her shawl from the rocking chair. She looks through the long windows onto the drive. A slim spill of sun parts the clouds and the trees are tipped with light. So are the heads of Noah and Tyler racing around the drive with the toy glider. A memory flares: Matthew and Jem at the same age. She blinks hard. Life has taken so much from her. Yet it has given, too, and for this reason she has never quite fallen apart. Her vicar, Aidan, would say it's God's grace, but as she's told him many times, she would have preferred Him to keep her family alive in the first place.

She forces herself to focus on the here and now, on Ram's protests about an apron.

'Mr Alan, I do not wear an apron at the restaurant. I am very happy without one!'

'But what about curry stains?' Al is incredulous. 'Your suits must be an outrage!'

She leaves them to their banter. 'I'm going to see if Esther needs help,' she tells them, but they're laughing so much they don't hear her.

Her daughter-in-law is in the dining room. The beautiful table is glossy with linen and silver. Brought back from India by Judith's father, it hasn't been decked like this for years.

'Esther, you're so clever. It looks amazing!' She leans on a chair to support herself. This wretched disease can weaken her with no warning. But nothing can steal her pleasure at seeing the handsome room ready for guests – flowers, candles, a Christmas tree. Best of all, a table for sixteen.

Even Esther looks happy. She stands back to admire her work, then begins to polish a knife. 'I had no idea it was so hard to clean silver,' she says, 'but I'm quite enjoying it, and it looks great. People are going to love today, Judith! How did you decide who to invite?'

Judith looks at the greenery her daughter-in-law has carefully arranged in a garland along the table's length. She sees the attention to detail and is touched. She ignores the question.

'Do you ever think about moving here?' she says. 'With me?'

Esther puts the knife down to complete a place setting. She moves it to the right a little, then moves it back. Outside, there's a shout followed by laughter. From below stairs a distant thump, and the drifting smell of spices.

'I would, Judith, I really would,' Esther says. 'I have to admit, I've always hated what the house stands for: the sense of entitlement, the status. But it was Matthew's home and it's beautiful. And the children love it.' She takes a breath. 'You're not getting any younger, though – forgive me – and without you, I don't know what would happen. I don't have your passion, couldn't do it myself. The counselling – you know how much I love it. I couldn't do both.'

Judith nods. She pulls the chair our and sits down heavily. She tries to imagine Ashdown House as a hotel or a health club. She has a mental image of bright-lipped receptionists and Formica. She shudders.

Esther is watching her, a fork in her hand. Judith draws herself up, pulls her shawl around her shoulders.

'To answer your question,' she says, keeping her voice level, 'I've invited the people I care about, those who matter to me most; those who are still alive, anyway.' An image of her dear friend

Anya comes to mind. How she would have loved today. But Anya, with her laugh and her mischievous eyes, is no more. She'd have been glad to know Kate is coming, though; that Judith keeps an eye on her daughter when she can.

'I didn't ask to be born into this family, you know,' she tells Esther. 'I never wanted status or influence. But I've tried to use it for good.'

There is a beat. Esther starts to buff the fork with a soft cloth. On the walls, from heavy frames, generations of Trentons turn up their noses at this speech, but Judith doesn't care. They are lucky to be here, in the house where their descendants live, instead of in a dusty antique shop.

She looks at her watch. She should go up and get changed. But Esther is picking up the place cards Judith spent yesterday writing in her best copperplate. Her daughter-in-law is near the window and, as her face is bathed in light, Judith thinks how much better she looks, how much happier. It makes her feel less guilty about manipulating their stay here. If Esther knew what she had done that day, it would affirm her view of her as an entitled old lady, arranging events to suit, to fit in with her plans. But her son's family were exhausted, burned out. They needed looking after and she and Al were the best people to do it. They've had such a lovely Christmas together, and both Esther and the children are better for it.

One day, she will confess, but not now.

'It will be good to see Dave again,' says Esther, putting one card down and picking up another one. 'But who is Duncan Greaves?' Her round face is curious as she holds the place card between a finger and thumb, perhaps wary of smudging it.

'Ah, Duncan.' Judith leans forward in the chair and puts her hands on the table. They look bony and old. She looks up. 'He's a dear man and a good friend. We met some years ago when I volunteered on the council's recycling stall. He often comes to the house. In the early days it was so he could talk through his ideas for new initiatives, but more recently it's been just to chat. He's very lonely.'

Esther puts the card down. She is smiling. 'You're so kind to people, Judith, so generous,' she says.

Judith stretches her fingers experimentally. The red nails look bright on the snowy cloth. She can't look at her daughter-in-law.

'What about Jan?' Esther says, lifting another card. There's a crash from the direction of the kitchen, and the sound of pop music. Al has put on Radio 2.

'Oh, you know Jan,' says Judith, 'the lady who comes on Tuesdays and Fridays. She's lovely. Her husband's not well and she doesn't get out much.'

'Oh, the cleaner!' says Esther and then blushes.

Judith leans back and puts her hands in her lap. She smiles. 'She's not just a cleaner,' she tells her. 'She's a carer, and a mum, and a daughter. And before that, an administrator.'

Esther pulls out a chair next to her mother-in-law and sits down. Her eyes are full of remorse.

'I'm sorry, I didn't mean it like that,' she says. She leans forward and takes one of Judith's hands in both of hers.

'I'm so grateful to you for having us, Judith,' she says. 'I was exhausted and in no place to move. I'd done nothing about Christmas. I didn't even sort the internet. The whole thing would have been a disaster. And being back here, well, it's been lovely. The hold-up was a blessing in disguise.'

She smiles. Judith cannot speak. Her awareness of Esther's hands, so warm, so *alive*, holding hers tenderly, almost undoes her.

The room holds its breath. Outside, the sound of another engine.

'I'd better go and get changed,' she says. She pushes Esther's hands gently away and pulls herself up.

'I invited Jem today,' she says, suddenly.

'Oh!' Esther's expression turns from surprise to hope. 'Do you think he'll come?'

'I don't know.' Judith pushes the chair in. It feels heavier than it used to. 'It will be lovely if he does. I've put him next to Al.' She motions towards the other end of the huge table.

Esther stands too. She starts to gather her things. 'What's he been doing all this time?'

Judith turns for the door. 'This and that. He prefers to be on the move. After, you know...'

Esther nods. 'Too much loss,' she says, 'can untether us.'

Judith's throat constricts. She wants this conversation to end, but it's her fault for mentioning Jem.

'It's not just that,' she says. 'Jem lived here his whole life. He never went away like Matthew did. And he resented the fact that, at the end of the day, everything was about this family, what we wanted. He needed to leave, but he's never settled anywhere. He comes back sometimes. I hope he'll come today.'

Esther's smile is sad, but she hurries Judith along. 'Go and rest for a bit,' she says. 'And don't come down until eleven. I'll get someone to help me with the drinks.'

Judith nods. 'Now who's the kind one?' she says.

After her rest, she pulls herself up from the four-poster bed with the support of a chair. She walks stiffly to the other side of the room where her green velvet hangs on the long mirror. She unhooks it, strokes the worn fabric redolent with age and memory. She would like to get changed here by the meagre warmth of the fire, but she must sit back on the bed to ease it over her legs. She twists her back painfully to see the zip in the mirror. She could ask any of the women downstairs for assistance, but this would be an admission of her need.

When she's dressed and on her feet, she is satisfied, in this darker corner of the room, with her reflection. She stands as straight as she can, turns sideways to examine herself. She finds she can do this dispassionately. The saggy arms, the skin around her neck, are signs that she has lived. Muscles that held placards and children, a neck that carried a level head. These have served her well. No one lives forever, though we're tricked into thinking so.

She smooths the soft velvet across her hips, swishes it around her ankles. There is something about a dress, much loved, long worn, that can lift the spirits. It remembers other versions of you, the young and lovely ones who walked tall, owned a room. She misses those women, but the dress helps her find a little of their youth, their confidence.

She rustles over to the dressing table by the window, sits to use the silver brush. She twists her long hair into a knot and fastens it with a tortoiseshell clip. She applies mascara, a slick of lipstick. The old face with its dips and shadows stares back, curious. *Who are you and where did Judith go?*

'I don't know,' she says aloud.

She gets up to find her shawl and sees people arriving outside. This room, with its huge window, is directly above the main door. She's always enjoyed watching people arrive while she dresses. She envies the next occupant that.

Her nephew's familiar figure, far too formal in his suit, is striding towards the door. It was lovely to see him for Christmas, to involve him in their celebrations. David looks up, perhaps guessing she is there. He seems about to wave but sees someone directly below and goes over. Frustratingly, she can't see who, despite hiding behind the heavy curtain and peering down at an angle.

The time has come. She takes one last look. *After today, everyone will know.* She nods at the old girl in the mirror, opens the door and makes her way down. It still gives her a thrill to walk down the grand staircase, despite having to avoid the splintered wood of the banisters.

The hallway is filled with family and friends chatting and toasting each other. Rosie and Ram are taking round trays of nibbles, the latter still wearing an apron. Sunil, Ram's son, has set up a cocktail bar on a table in the window. Noah and Tyler are crawling after the baby, supervised by Ruby and Mia. She catches her granddaughter's eye and blows a kiss. Ruby salutes. What a blessing the girl is.

No one sees her come down and she is grateful. But as she reaches the bottom step, Aidan appears.

'Your ladyship!' He offers his hand while giving a bow, and she giggles, like a girl. She gives him a kiss.

'I didn't think you went anywhere without your dog collar,' she says.

He smiles. 'I'm branching out. Trying to live a bit.'

'Oh?' She smiles at him. He really is the loveliest man and has supported her through so much. His face, she decides, reflects his kindness, his gentle optimism. He is why, these last dreadful months, she's started going to church and has found, if not faith exactly, a certain dogged hope. Surely there is somewhere better. Before, her idea of heaven was akin to the ceiling of the Sistine Chapel – striking but inaccessible. But, after weekly exposure to Aidan's gentle sermons, she thinks more of a house on a hill, lighted rooms, a welcome.

'I was in a train accident the other day,' Aidan tells her. 'It changes things. By the way I met a lovely woman, a writer. Kim Franklin. If any of the organisations you support need one, let me know.'

'I will,' she says, mentally storing this away. She pats his arm. 'Is Amy here yet? I haven't seen her for ages.'

'She's over there,' he replies, pointing.

She looks and there is Aidan's twin sister on the other side of the hall, talking to Jan. That's good. Both carers. Mutual support.

Aidan leans closer, pointing towards a couple by the fireplace. She can smell his aftershave.

Judith looks past him to where her nephew is standing, and has a jolt of surprise. Not because David is chatting animatedly with Anya's daughter, but because their posture suggests they have not just met.

'Oh,' she says, 'I didn't know David knew Kate!'

The vicar nods. 'They became friends on a train apparently,' he says.

The bell rings as they go for lunch. In the dining room, arm in arm with Jan and Amy, Judith sees Ram has done them proud. The hostess trollies, unused for years, are either side of the long table and a mouth-watering smell of curry fills the room. Rosie has set out her desserts along the length of the buffet – pies, meringues, trifle – flanked by perfect cones of strawberries. Esther's beautiful table decorations, branches of fir and twists of ivy, recall dinner parties of old, she at one end, George at the other. She is sitting in her usual place from where, with her head to one side of the line of flickering candles, she can see David picking up his name card at the other end. His surprise is evident.

Al slides into place next to her, averting his gaze; Rosie calls the children. Kate and Jan are trying to persuade Ram to sit down. They point at his apron, which he was clearly persuaded to wear after all. He flushes and starts to remove it as they drag him towards a chair.

There is a tap on her arm.

'Judith, I just answered the door,' Esther says quietly. Her eyes are warm. 'You'd better come.'

Judith stands with difficulty and calls above the clamour. 'Aidan will say grace, then go ahead and eat. We'll be back in a minute.' She taps Al's arm and he looks up.

'We?'

She inclines her head ever so slightly. He gets up and takes her arm.

It's cold in the hallway, the door recently opened, warmth sucked from the fireplace. But when she sees he's come, it's warm enough. Al smothers a gasp. He stops by the staircase, wary.

But Jem has put down his cello and his rucksack in readiness. While father and son embrace, Judith must look away. Funny how you can survive years of your own pain but be undone by another's.

When they've finished, she offers Jem her cheek but is swept up in a hug that could break her.

Al watches, his heart in his eyes.

'I do know what you two got up to when I went away,' Jem says, but his voice is warm.

They turn, Jem's arm around Judith's waist.

His father nods. 'How did you get here today?'

Jem is moving his cello, leaning it with care against the side of the staircase.

'I had a lift from Pat,' he says. 'I've been staying at The Heights in return for playing over Christmas. The clients loved it!'

His eyes are bright, the old spark back. It's taken time, but then, he and Matthew were close. Despite being brought up at opposite ends of the estate hierarchy, Matthew in the big house, Jem in the gatehouse, they were the same age with identical interests. Both only children, they were like brothers. Until Matthew went away, and Jem's mother died. Then Matthew had become ill too.

To lose his mother and his brother, in a place he was already starting to resent, had required drastic action. Jem's was to leave.

Back in the dining room, those who know Jem – which is most of them – let out a cheer. A chair is pulled out, a glass poured. Ram rushes around finding hot plates to fill with food.

David and Kate stack up the fire. And together they eat and drink and celebrate.

As she eats, Judith watches Al and Jem, whose faces are flushed with relief and alcohol in the same places. On her other side, Jan tells her about her new client, Mike, and she tells Jan how he and his wife bought land from her to build their house. There is laughter from the other end where David, Kate and Duncan are sitting. The children are clustered around Rosie, who is teaching them origami with napkins. The atmosphere is lovely, everything she hoped for.

During coffee, with the brightness of the day fading beyond the window and her heart knocking in her chest, Judith decides it's time. But before she can call them to order, Jem gets up and returns with his cello. He pulls out a chair, sits, nestles its neck in the hollow of his shoulder. Hauntingly, he begins to play.

One by one, they fall silent, captive to Bach's brutal tenderness. Even the children are quiet. No one looks at anyone, because music can slice you open to reveal the nakedness within. It carries them back to places they have been to, people they have loved. Then forward with hope to the unfilled days ahead. It lowers them and it lifts them, a seamless ebb and flow during which their hearts leave their bodies in search of heaven.

The notes fall away like water; the spell is broken. The room shifts and yawns, but before it can resume its chatter, the mood is changed again.

Judith watches with admiration and amusement as Jem's dancing fingers launch into *Auld Lang Syne*. *How skilled a musician is, how powerful*, she thinks, *like God*. In the space of a few minutes, he has disarmed the room twice.

People leap up, circle the table, grasp each other's hands. They pump their arms – Judith loudly reminding them she's old and frail – throw their heads back, sing.

Sing away the old year with its pleasures and regrets, sing in the New Year, its days unlived as yet.

Judith looks round at her people, her tribe. At Ram and Jan, Ruby, Esther and Noah. At Aidan and Amy and Mia and Kate and Rosie, at Tyler and Baby Elsie. At David and Duncan and, of course, Al and Jem.

And in an instant, she changes what she will tell them.

Perhaps it's the wine or the music or the fire, a smile in the dying embers of the day, but she's filled with that old anticipation. New Year, new start, so many possibilities. She will thank them for coming, say how grateful she is for all of them, how she wanted to say thank you. Then she will remind them that no one lasts forever, not even her.

She'll say how she hopes the house will be used for good when she's gone. The family won't want it – she'll try not to look at Esther at this point – but she would turn in her grave if it were a hotel, or even worse, one of those health clubs. She would love it to be useful, to make a difference to the community. But she has no idea how.

'You,' she'll say, 'my trusted friends, will you help me put together a plan for something good? Something of value for the future?'

In the end, her moment comes easily. Jem finishes the song to a round of applause and they fall into their seats exhausted. Dear David raises a glass to her generosity and, God bless them, they toast her health. Then they call for a speech.

She smiles and struggles to her feet, assisted by Al and Jan. She stands as tall as she can and gazes along the candlelit length of the table towards the window. Outside it's nearly dark. It will be a clear night and soon the glitter of countless stars will light the way to dawn.

Anyone can see darkness. It takes courage to look for light. But light is a curious thing. It can slip away when you think you've caught it, revealing not what you hoped for but something as precious – the invisible ties that bind us all.

It amazes her that time has something to teach her, even now. Perhaps especially now. In the winter of your life, light comes slowly then all at once.

And winter light, in all its forms, is the most beautiful of all.

Winter Lights

Two Years Later

Ground-breaking new care home opens in Henford

The Henford Herald *is pleased to report that a new, ground-breaking facility for respite care is about to open in the area. In partnership with the council, services will include support for not only those with long-term conditions but also for their carers.*

Managing Director Duncan Greaves, the council's former head of Recycling and Waste, told us: 'Due to the care crisis, family members are much more likely to be responsible for the burden of care, and it is now widely acknowledged that long-term support for carers is a necessity, not a luxury. We are proud to be able to offer an innovative two-tier care system at Ashdown House.'

Historic seat of the Trenton family, this stately home in the heart of the forest was left to a charitable trust established by the late Lady Trenton.

Judith Trenton, who passed away last year, set up the trust towards the end of her life, dreaming of 'a beacon of excellence in convalescent, respite and end-of-life support for those giving and receiving care.' The organisation was set up with money from the Trenton estate.

David Trenton, Chief Executive of the care facility and nephew of the former owner, invited several well-known and widely respected individuals in our community to sit on the trust's governing body. These include Ram Singh, retired former owner of the hugely popular Masala Ram restaurant and cocktail bar, Rosie Ferguson, proprietor of the Olive Tree, and Reverend Aidan Shand, of the parish church. Amy Lane, part-time teacher at Blackdown Primary School, has accepted the post of clerk to the governors.

Ashdown House has been renovated to create a series of warm, light spaces while preserving its unique character. To restore many of the original features, the trust has employed stonemasons, joiners, furniture restorers and carpenters. Local man Mike Derrick, who built his own house in the forest and is an expert carpenter, spent months touching up the many metres of wood comprising the hall and grand staircase despite recently becoming disabled. An old friend of Lady Trenton, who lives on former estate land, Mr Derrick told us it was a privilege to be involved in such a worthwhile endeavour. His partner, Jan Dixon, agrees.

'If only I'd had access to a place like this when my husband was alive,' she said. 'Both Mike and I have experienced first-hand the ravaging effects of dementia and the lack of support available for sufferers, to say nothing of their carers. We love to think that the work here will offer others a level of support that will make a real difference to their lives.'

State-of-the-art facilities at the care home include a heated swimming pool, on-site counselling, qualified nursing staff and a cordon bleu cook, the aforementioned Rosie Ferguson, owner of the Olive Tree café and restaurant. Lisa Goodwood is the full-time administrator and a volunteer-based support programme has been set up, organised by Ruby Trenton, granddaughter of the founder. It is understood that music therapy courses will also be available, which research shows to have had a huge impact on *those in care, particularly dementia patients. Jeremy Penfold, who was brought up on the estate, is currently undergoing training for this role.*

One of the first beneficiaries of respite care at the centre will be David Trenton's wife Kate, whose disabled sister currently lives in a Henford care home. Kate told us, 'This is going to make such a difference to my life. I have spent the last couple of years travelling up and down from London to see my sister. Frankly, I was exhausted. The opportunity for Megan to come and live here where I can spend quality time with her, as well as get the support I need, is such a gift.'

In her will, Judith Trenton left considerable funds for the day-to-day operation of the care home. This carefully orchestrated and innovative provision for vulnerable people and their carers is testament to Judith's lifetime of service in the community. Over the years she has championed numerous causes, raised thousands of pounds and volunteered herself.

Lady Trenton left specific instructions as to the management and organisation of the new care home, including its name.

The Henford Herald *is therefore proud to sponsor the new Winter Lights Foundation Trust. We wish its members every success for the future.*

Article by Kim Franklin
Acting Assistant Editor

Acknowledgements

A child once asked me, 'If you wasn't a good writer, what would you be?' After correcting his grammar, I said I'd have been a bad writer. I explained I would always have been a writer – it's all I've ever wanted to do, though I wasn't much good to begin with. But I learned from others, I told him, and I got better.

He put his head on one side and said, 'Like I'm a rubbish goalie but want to play for England, so Aaron helps me?'

'Yes,' I said, 'just like that.'

One of the reasons I've ended up being a not-bad writer is the incredible support I've had from family, friends and writing companions. I mentioned most of them at the end of my first book and my thanks to these wonderful people still stands.

Thanks also to Rob Hustwayte for answering questions, in his professional capacity, for one of the stories. And for always having a smile on his face.

I'd like to thank fellow Fairlight author Sarah Butler for her advice before I wrote this book. Also, for friendship, walks, cake and gardening tips which lighten my life.

I'll always be grateful to the Incomprehensibles and the Reckless Ones (long story) who give almost daily encouragement in writing and in life. You bring light on dark days.

Many thanks to my lovely editor Sarah Shaw, who has been a joy to work with. Huge thanks also to Louise Boland, for supporting me and believing in my books, and to Greer Claybrook, Swetal Agrawal, Beccy Fish and Mo Fillmore, who all work so hard on behalf of their writers. Thank you, Beccy, for a gorgeous cover which showcases the stories so well.

I'm so grateful for Laura Shanahan's involvement with *Winter Lights*. Thank you, Laura, for continuing to cheer me on.

Fran Hill remains a daily source of wisdom and LOLs (can't believe I said LOLs. In print too).

I couldn't spend so much time writing without the support of my brilliant husband, Steve, and lovely family. Thank you all.

Finally, to my grandchild (who will have arrived by the time this book is out), I will say this: the world is beautiful and terrible and, at times, very dark. But there's always light for those who look. Never stop looking...

About the Author

Deborah Jenkins is a freelance writer and primary teacher who has worked in schools in the UK and abroad. Her novel Braver published with Fairlight Books in June 2022, and was shortlisted for the Writers' Guild of Great Britain Best First Novel Award and the Society of Authors ADCI Literary Prize. She has written several educational textbooks, as well as articles for the TES online and Guardian Weekend, among other publications. Her short fiction has appeared in magazines and anthologies, and she has also published a novella, *The Evenness of Things*. She lives in Sussex and enjoys reading, walking, gardening, travel and good coffee.

DEBORAH JENKINS

Braver

Hazel has never felt normal. Struggling with OCD and anxiety, she isolates herself from others and sticks to rigid routines in order to cope with everyday life. But when she forms an unlikely friendship with Virginia, a church minister, Hazel begins to venture outside her comfort zone.

Having rebuilt her own life after a traumatic loss, Virginia has become the backbone of her community, caring for those in need and mentoring disadvantaged young people. Yet a shock accusation threatens to unravel everything she has worked for.

Told with warmth, compassion and gentle humour, *Braver* is an uplifting story about the strength that can be drawn from friendship and community.

'*Utterly human, and deeply compassionate*'
—Loree Westron, author of *Missing Words*

'*A feel-good story of vulnerability, friendship and community... This heartwarming book left me with a warm glow.*'
—*LoveReading*

JENNA WARREN
The Moon and Stars

Matthew Capes, struggling with chronic stage fright, has not sung in front of an audience for ten years. A classical tenor with a magnificent voice, he only dares sing late at night on the empty stage of the Moon and Stars theatre.

When Matthew's old singing partner Angela – who just so happens to be the woman of his dreams – gets back in touch and offers him the chance to perform in a nationwide tour, his low self-esteem and anxiety stand in the way. But Matthew has a plan: he will sing in the shadows while his handsome and charismatic friend Ralph takes to the stage with Angela. What could go wrong?

Loosely inspired by *The Phantom of the Opera*, this warm and witty debut novel is the perfect read for fans of David Nicholls.

'*A thoroughly uplifting story, full of light, shade, and lots of great music*'
—Matson Taylor, author of *The Miseducation of Evie Epworth*

'*Romantic and engaging*'
—*The People's Friend*